For Marjorie, Steven and Ian

ON MY WAY WEEPING

On My Way Weeping

a frontier woman's story

Steve McGiffen

BLACK ACE BOOKS

First published in 1994 by
Black Ace Books, Ellemford, Duns
Berwickshire, TD11 3SG, Scotland

© Steve McGiffen 1994

Typeset in Scotland by Black Ace Editorial

Printed in Great Britain by Antony Rowe Ltd
Bumper's Farm, Chippenham, SN14 6QA

A CIP catalogue record for this book
is available from the British Library

Hardback ISBN   1–872988–21–0
Paperback ISBN   1–872988–26–1

CONTENTS

Turn our captivity, O Lord, as the rivers in the south.
They that sow in tears, shall reap in joy.
He that now goeth on his way weeping, and
beareth forth good seed, shall doubtless come
again with joy, and bring his sheaves with him.

Psalm 126

1

Spring, 1866

Nate opened the door that day, didn't walk in, just stood there in the doorway and right away I knew who it was and he stood, waiting for Ma to go to him I suppose and put her arms around him. I wanted to do that myself but knew if I did Swann would more than is likely give me a beating for it even though Nate was my brother I hadn't seen in more than ten years since I was a little girl and they put him away for killing Pa.

So Nate just stood there.

No-one knew he was coming. Annabel and James stood and looked at him and then they could kind of feel Swann rising up like the thick hair on the back of a dog and that made James cry and I would've gone to him but I could not move there was no air in the room or air like water and even though winter had hardly passed it was hotter than Hell's kitchen. And then Annabel took him and held him to her, so James stopped crying and snuffled into Annabel's dress the way he does.

Swann could see Nate weren't armed but of course didn't know him from Adam and so picked up his rifle and said,

'Who in Hell are you, mister?'

Ma turned a little way toward Swann and she said, so you could hardly hear,

'It's okay, it's Nathan.'

So Swann stacked his gun but he did not smile nor shake hands nor go into the yard to kill a chicken. Ma did not put her arms around Nate at all but she did put coffee on the table for him and some beans and corn-bread.

You could see Nate wasn't happy but I couldn't say a word to him. Ma said,

'You out legal?' and Nate answered her,

'Sure.' He said, 'I tried to get word to you with a fellow thought he might be passing this way but I guess it didn't work out.'

Ma said,

'Who ever passes this way?'

She looked hard into Nate's face, almost like she'd asked him a real question and was waiting for his answer. Then she said,

'You should've written. I could've had Mrs Packer from the trading boat read it to me.'

But Nate just scowled into his beans. Swann should've been going back out to the field then but he stayed. Ma said,

'It don't matter, so long as you're out and free and they won't be looking for you.'

'I ain't been in jail in four years, Ma,' Nate answered her. 'They let me out to fight.'

Then there was a kind of awkwardness, but Nate smiled over at me when Ma stepped back to the stove to fill up his coffee cup and he said,

'Well, Sissy, you sure done some growing while I been breaking rocks and getting myself shot at by them Southern boys.'

And I wanted to smile and speak and kiss him but there was Swann, watching me, and I daren't say a word. So Nate said,

'Aren't you going to introduce me to these here, who I suppose is my niece and nephew?'

I coughed and swallowed and looked over at Swann and Swann wasn't looking at me mean so I said,

'Annabel, James, this here's your Uncle Nathan,' and James looked at him quick and then buried his face in Annabel's dress again and started to cry. Annabel carried on looking at him with her big, round eyes, and held on tight to James.

There was some more talk. Nate asked about when his dog Pirate had died and Ma said Pirate'd died of old age about five years back.

'We had to put him to sleep to save him from suffering,' Ma said, and I looked at her but she pressed her lips together like it was true if she said it was true, and I guess it was true at that, at least some of it was, in the words of it.

Nate knew about Swann and about Annabel and James because Ma had Mrs Packer write him for us, three times in the ten years he was away she done that, though the letters took more than a year to find him. Anyway, she couldn't tell much with someone she hardly knew writing it down for her, is what she said to me about those letters. I didn't know why that meant she couldn't tell about Pirate, at least the way she told it to Nate then, which wasn't really how I remembered it though.

The rest of the evening Swann did not leave the house but sat cleaning his guns and hunting gear. Nobody spoke much.

Nate went for a walk around the farm to see what changes had been made, I guess. Swann must've seemed straight away like an animal to Nate but it was true he could work, never did a thing but work, he had this terrible energy made him want to work all the time, so the place was looking good and we ate well. Course we always looked like beggars because Swann would not let us spend money on clothes or anything. Ma and me had to make everything we needed, we didn't mind that, but he would not let us buy good cloth, or enough cloth of any kind to last out the year decent.

We went to bed early, like always, and Swann had to use me like always. Nate was forced to sleep in the barn because there wasn't room for him in the house. I could've made him a bed but I was scared to say.

Next morning Swann was up, first light, and out to the field, but Nate was still getting used to not being in jail or the army and he slept in the loft of the barn until the sun had started to climb.

I remember him coming to the door again, he stood there with the sun behind him and Ma saw him, she didn't say a thing but she started to fry some ham and biscuits. Nate watched her and he looked at me and the kids who were fooling around on the floor with some wooden spoons I'd given them to play with. They looked around and I thought James was going to cry again but Annabel said, like a real little lady,

'Good morning, Uncle Nathan,' and I have never seen a man smile broader.

I smiled too and Nate said,

'It sure is a good morning, Annabel.' Then he went out to the pump to wash up.

When he came back Ma put his breakfast in front of him. She tried to conjure up a smile but you could see it was hard work. I was watching her real close and I could see into her, I could see inside her what she was thinking.

Ma don't lie that she knows she is lying, and neither does Nathan, but they both have the same thing, he took it from her I guess, that they can believe things are true when they ain't; and this makes it awful hard to understand what they are saying to each other. It's like the words they form with their mouths are the same as the words they form with their minds, but the pictures behind the words in their minds aren't the same, always, as the pictures the world gave them to store away there. It would be all right I guess if I only loved one of them, then I could just take their side and believe in what they believe in.

But loving them both is what makes it so hard.

After a while Ma said to Nate,

'Well, son, I guess you'll have some plans now they let you out that place and out the army too.'

But Nate had a mouth full of biscuit and he couldn't speak, just looked at her with a look, I hadn't seen it before but I got to recognise it, like he thought Ma was crazy. Then when he'd emptied his mouth enough to speak he said,

'What kind of plans, Ma?'

Ma was standing in front of him, she was clearing up the kitchen end of the room because everyone had eaten breakfast and there would be no more feeding till noon, and she looked at Nate, like she knew him real well, like he had not been away at all. She said,

'Nathan, you can see how it is here.'

And he just looked.

'Why did you come back?' She said it with a break in her voice like she was going to cry, and she put her hand up to her face. Even the children had gone quiet, now. I didn't want them to hear no more, so I shooed them out into the yard and told Annabel to take James and hunt up some eggs.

Nate waited until the kids were gone, and he said,

'I come back for my farm, Ma.'

I knew then that something bad had walked in with Nathan, following on his heels like a mean dog. And I thought about Swann and how he had known it too, in his own way.

15

Ma dried her hands on her apron. She said,

'Nathan I'm glad you survived your years in jail and whatever battles you been in. I'm proud you done your piece to save the Union, too. You look healthy for a man's been through what you been through. You ain't no giant but you look like you can work. But now I seen you, satisfied myself you ain't dead nor gone crazy, I think you ought to eat up your ham and biscuits, take a loaf of that fresh bread standing on the stove there, and head out of here, maybe up to Oregon—'

Then Ma started to cry, holding her hand up to her face, bending in on herself like there was nothing outside of her that she could trust or even understand.

Nate only sat, he looked like he did not know what was happening to him. He looked at me, but I couldn't help him. I had begun to feel this fear, wanted to hunker down behind the barn over toward the field like I did when I was a little girl. It wasn't a fear like the fear of Swann and the way he would beat me and use me, wasn't a fear like that, which was a routine kind of a fear I had every day. This fear got inside me, right inside to where I really am. The other fear, the Swann fear, that was just there on my surface, in the parts of me he liked to hurt, in my skin and my face and the places where he would use me.

'Do you know what in Hell is going on here, Sissy?' Nathan asked me, but he didn't really ask me like he wanted an answer. He said it all for Ma, the question thrown at me, the profanity, the lie in it all.

He carried on sitting there at the table, even though I wanted him so much to get up and put his arms round Ma and for her to let him, even though I wanted that more than I had ever wanted anything in my life, even though I wanted it so much I was sure I would be granted it, he just sat there, and she stood, near to him in distance, but not touching or being together at all.

Then Nate said,

'Ma, I come back here to work my farm, that I've thought about and dreamt about all the time I was in that stinking jail, and all the time I was being froze and baked and half-starved and used for target practice these last four years.'

Ma turned on him, real fast, she looked like a snake turning on him and she said,

'It ain't your farm, Nathan, it's my farm, d'you hear?'

Nate looked up at her with a shocked and kind of sorry look, and he said,

'I know that Ma. I know it's your farm. But if I last longer'n you then it'll be my farm, won't it, and I have to start planning and working for that day right now.'

Ma stood at the other end of the table from Nate and she looked right at him and said,

'First thing is, you don't inherit a farm by killing your Pa, even in this godforsaken country—'

But Nate interrupted her, he looked like she'd took out a rifle and shot him in the heart, and he said,

'Ma, that ain't true. I wasn't convicted of murdering Pa—'

'You killed him all the same.'

'I killed him, yeah.'

Now I thought Nathan was going to cry. He is not a big man. Swann was three of him. But when he sat in front of Ma that morning he looked like a child, like James when you scold him. He was quiet for a minute or so, maybe waiting for Ma to speak, but she didn't say a word. He even looked up at me, once, but I didn't think I ought to break the silence. Then he said,

'I killed him after I couldn't take no more. You know that.

17

I killed him when he come at me the way he used to, I didn't mean to kill him, all I did was pick up the nearest thing I could lay my hands on, just to keep him off me.'

I thought Ma would hit him, but she hit the table instead. I ain't never seen her so angry. She shouted at him,

'How dare you repeat all those lies to me now. Oh, God, why did you give me a son like this, is it because I ain't no good?' And she screamed up at the roof, 'Is it?'

Nate looked at her, quiet and calm on the outside, but I could feel what was inside him, like he was falling and falling down a well with no bottom to it. I wanted to reach out and catch him and hold him tight so he couldn't fall no more nor come to harm, but I couldn't reach him and he was falling too fast, the air was rushing up past him as he fell and fell.

And Nate said, without raising his voice,

'I don't know what you're talking about, Ma. I come back to my home and family is all.'

I looked at Ma's face and I thought I could see some love in it, fighting with the hardness she'd built to protect herself from what Nathan had done.

But just then Swann appeared at the door. He must've heard Ma shouting to God. He didn't speak to me or Ma, didn't ask what was going on, he just walked over to Nate and said to him, real quiet in that way I know which is worse than his shouting and cussing,

'If you've finished your breakfast, I think you better get on out of here.'

There wasn't much Nate could've done. He could see that if he tried to argue with Swann, Swann would've killed him. But he turned his head toward Ma and said,

'You gonna let him do this to me, Ma? You gonna let him turn me off my own farm?'

Swann hit him across the face, not with his fist but with

the back of his hand, like he'd hit a child or a woman, like he usually hit me, and Nate fell back off his chair. He wasn't hurt bad, but he got hisself up off the floor and walked out, didn't say another word or even give a look to any of us. As he walked toward the door I noticed James standing just outside on the porch, holding a stick he'd found to play with and watching, quiet for once, just watching. Nate didn't seem to see him, he walked past him, back out into the sun, paying him no more heed than he had me.

I thought I had learned but when Nate walked out like that I couldn't stop myself, I put my head in my hands and cried and cried, for Nate and for Ma and for me as well, and Swann took hold of my wrist and twisted it and told me to shut up, and when I kept on crying he hit me across the face like he had hit Nate, then he got hisself some coffee off the stove and went on back to the field.

2

Nate

I knew Nate was there all the time. I could feel him there, even though I didn't see him, cause he took care to keep well hid.

I had to wait till Saturday night, which is when Swann would go into town to get drunk and gamble our spare change away, not that he ever gambled or drunk away what we really needed. Nobody ever went hungry here, like I said.

He liked to go with whores there, too, so he could tell me the ways he used them and make me do the dirty things he had them do. I didn't care, because Saturday night was my time, too, it was the only time I got when I knew Swann was not going to beat me or use me or make me work. Course, he always made sure I had work to do, plenty of work, but he would be away all night and sleep it off most of Sunday, so I always could grab an hour or two for myself on Saturday night.

It was so sweet to be able to sleep alone and know that, at least until first light and sometimes, in the summer when it comes light early, for long after that, I would not have to look upon Swann or smell his awful stink in the bed next to me. It was good, too, to be able to play with my babies and hold them warm against me without having to worry that Swann would come in and do or say something mean, without having to feel his eyes on us and feel his hate of our love, without for a little while having to wonder how many years he would give Annabel before he began to use her like he used me.

But the best time was not when I could sleep alone in a clean bed, nor even when I could just be happy for once with my babies, the best time was the time between when Annabel would go to sleep and when I couldn't keep my eyes open no more, then I could sit before the stove if it was winter, or out in the yard looking over toward the field and the mountains, and I could think and think and think. I could try, though it weren't easy, to look inside myself like I could look inside Ma and Nate and most anybody, but like I say it weren't easy, and it still ain't. Sometimes all I see inside there is a great whiteness, like a blizzard in the far north country in the dead of the year when the ground's too hard to dig a grave and the dead lie unburied. All I see is black lines like the trees when all the life has gone, only it ain't gone it's just lying sleeping. I can look at a tree in winter and if I look real hard I can see the green spring way down deep. So I tried to look down deep into myself and see the spring there, but it was awful hard.

And then, Nathan was there, living up on the mountain, feeling his freedom after all those years in the darkness. When I looked up to the mountains and the forest I could feel him there, feel his love and freedom and the sorrow of his loss and something else, too, something hidden. Even when Nate was up close there was a shut place in him like there was in Ma and I guess in me too.

I had to see him. I knew he was up there, waiting for me to come, that no-one else would come if I didn't. So I waited one Saturday night, two weeks after he had arrived home I think it was, I waited till James was sound asleep and Annabel settled, and I said to Ma,

'I'm going out to take some air.'

Ma was trying to sew in fading light and she didn't even look up. I guess she liked to be on her own a little too. So I took a shotgun in case of bears or Indians and I set out, scared as I was and wishing Pirate was beside me to give me courage.

It is about a mile to the forest and about another mile to the place where the narrow band of trees thins out and the land begins to climb and grow rocky. That is where I guessed Nate would be, but that night I guessed wrong. I sat on a big rock and I called out to him as it grew dark. I heard my voice bounce around the hillsides but I did not hear Nate answer, not with my mind either.

I waited about a half hour, but I knew right away he wasn't there. I knew he'd been there, all right, but it was like he'd gone away, I could feel his absence as real as I'd felt him being there in the days before.

Sitting in the dark out there, I felt the strength grow inside me. I walked back through the woods in the darkness, but I didn't feel scared no more. When you have lived as I have lived you don't fear fairy tales, and I thought if a bear took me it would be the Lord's mercy and I knew Ma would take care of my babies. As for the Indians, no man, white or red, could use a woman worse than Swann used me.

I got word from Nate a couple days after. It was the day we all looked forward to, the day the trading boat would come up the river and stop at our landing.

You wouldn't always know exactly the day but you could guess when it was due and start to wait. You could even watch for it if you could think of chores to do down by the river. When it came it would let out a long blast of its whistle, loud enough to echo off the mountains, and me and the kids would run down to the river with Ma coming on behind us grumbling that she was an old woman and couldn't keep up.

Before Pa died there was a boat, though not so big and fancy as the one we had by then, and folks would come from other farms around, folks that lived away from the river, and they would use our landing to meet it and buy what they needed and trade their eggs and other stuff. But since that happened, no-one ever came near our farm, they would go further up river, out of their way and across more miles of harder country, just to avoid the bad luck we was supposed to bring, to meet the boat someplace else. So the boatman and his son and sometimes his wife and maybe a passenger or two he might have along, they would be the only people we would see from one year to the next. We got all our news from them, about comings and goings in the area, if there were any bad men or hostile Indians riding nearby, and news about the War, too, and other things going on out in the world.

Swann did all our town dealing, but the boat served a lot of our needs. Ma would bring eggs, mostly, and sometimes cheese she had made or butter, and we would exchange them for cloth, things to eat we couldn't grow ourselves, oil for the lamp. We had enough to get by with what we could keep out of Swann's hands, although I know Ma especially would have liked more to spend on clothing us all. If I ever said anything to Ma about how little he left us, though, she would ask me to remember how we got along before he came.

The day he brought the message from Nate, the boatman had some toys I'd never seen before, that if you pulled two ends of a piece of string, this coloured piece of wood, round it was, in the middle of the string and with all kinds of colours, this wood would spin and spin and the colours

23

would disappear and it would just be white. He weren't selling them, but if you spent more'n two bits you got one of these with what you bought, it was so's the children would get on to their mammas to spend two bits I guess. So Ma needed some pieces of stuff and leather to mend some of Swann's overalls and some other things and she spent near thirty cents, and the boatman give her this wood and string thing and her face lit up at the sight of it, on account of she had had one when she was a little girl, her Pa had made it. So Ma had to rush off just like she was a little girl again and show the toy to Annabel and teach her how to work it, to make it spin so all the colours would go.

Annabel and James were at the other side of the boat with the boatman's son, who was whittling a real-looking Indian canoe from a piece of pine, so Ma went off to show them the toy. I stayed with the boatman because I had a penny and thought I would spend it on a piece of candy I could eat with my babies on Saturday night while Swann was in town.

As soon as Ma was out of earshot the man said, real low, and all the time shooting looks around to make sure we were alone,

'You're Elizabeth, aren't you?'

I nearly didn't know because it had been so long since anyone called me by my given name, Ma called me Sissy or 'child' if I hadn't pleased her and Swann never called me nothing. But when the boatman asked me I knew right away why he was asking and I come back to myself and nodded at him, just a little nod as if, cause that is how I felt even though I knew Swann was a good mile away and Ma was at the other side of the boat, just like I thought someone might be watching me. Then the man said,

'I got a message for you from your brother Nate. He's working over to the Turner place, you know?'

I nodded again.

24

'He says, can you get away and meet him anytime, some place near here?'

Then the boatman froze and gave a little look over my shoulder. I turned around and there was Ma coming back round the end of the boat with Annabel, and Annabel was holding on to the toy and wanting to show it to me. I said to the boatman, before Ma got near enough to hear,

'Sure, tell him Tennant's Rock, any Saturday night, any time between sundown and when they ain't no light left.'

And then there was Annabel, twirling that toy round and round and squealing and laughing and the boatman was packing things away and getting ready to move off and I had to hide the candy in my skirts so's it would be a surprise for Annabel and help to settle her Saturday night.

When I got to Tennant's rock, just as the light was beginning to fade, and I come out of the trees where the forest thins out and the river bends, I could see Nate sitting on top of that rock overlooking the waterfall that splashes down the hillside and makes the little stream that runs into the river there, sitting high right on top of it, and I thought what would've happened if Swann had discovered us and it was him coming out of the wood now, his rifle in his hand and Nate sitting there like a baby fawn don't know no better, like the one we ate this time last year, that Swann told Ma, laughing, had just about stuck its little nose down the barrel of his gun.

Something made me not call out to Nate, it wasn't fear we would be heard but something else, I wanted to be watching him without he knew I was there. I wanted to know him when nobody was watching him and he was just sitting, waiting for me, his thoughts not locked up like you have to when someone is watching you.

But when I come up near enough to hear, I thought there

must be someone else there with him, I could hear his voice, low, like he was murmuring to hisself, and then I could see pretty well that there wasn't no-one with him, and I thought the spell in jail must've robbed him of some of his wits. I was climbing up to him, and even though he had his back to me I was sure he would've heard me, the smile was waiting inside my face to come out when he turned around, but he just kept on sitting there, kind of stooped over, murmuring in that way to hisself.

Course, I don't remember what he was saying but I can tell it anyway, because what he was saying wasn't coming like I thought from his own head, but from the book he was reading, which I hadn't never seen no-one doing that, except I had seen people looking at newspapers in town before Swann come, and I had seen some books and newspapers on the trading boat but, not being able to read, I hadn't paid them no mind. Ma could read some but she never did and she wouldn't teach me, though I begged her to once or twice.

What I heard Nate saying, when I still couldn't see the book, convinced me, and it broke my heart, that my brother was crazy, because at that time I couldn't make no sense of it. So he says,

'That's why they gets cut up and marked so. If they behaved themselves they wouldn't.' And then Nate let out a little snort.

I didn't move, I froze, still thinking I was watching a crazy person, and wondering if he'd gotten me to come out here so's he could kill me, and all kinds of things like that. I remember thinking of a song Ma had taught me, where the devil takes on the form of a handsome man, Pa used to sing it she said, and he lures seven girls down to the river or the lake or some place and he drowns six of them, but the seventh one tricks him and pushes him into the water and escapes. And I wondered whether the devil had possessed Nate and if that was why he killed Pa and now he was going to kill me. Maybe what I could hear, I thought, was the same as prayers, only they was prayers to the devil.

Then he said,

'That is to say, the Lord made 'em men, and it's a hard squeeze getting 'em down into beasts, said the drover drily.'

And Nate stopped again, leaving me, who couldn't see no sense in what he was saying, wondering whether I should turn around quick and go back into the forest and home to my babies. It was getting dark now, with the last rays of sun reflecting off the wide still river, and breaking up in the whirlpools where the little stream joined up with it, just this fading light to help me pick my way through the trees and see whether there were any signs that what was sitting up there was really Satan or his servant.

Nate said,

'Bright niggers isn't no kind of vantage to their masters,' then he stopped again, and he kept saying things now weren't even words, he kept saying something like 'con . . . cont . . . cont', and then he finally got it and went on, 'continued the other, well . . . oh Hell . . . '

He stopped for a minute, and I was wondering whether I should call to him, but he went on again, a little louder now, like I had been wrong and he was talking to someone, maybe someone out of my sight just the other side of him. He said,

'What's the use o' talents and them things if you can't use 'em on yourself? Why, all the use they make on't is to get round you. I've had one or two of these fellers, and I jest sold 'em down the river. I knew I'd got to lose 'em, first or last, if I didn't.'

Nate bust out laughing, so's his shoulders shook and he sure sounded crazy, and he said,

'Better send up to the Lord to make you a set, and leave out their souls entirely, said the drover.'

Then he didn't laugh no more, and I realised he'd been reading from a book, because he put the book to one side of him and looked over to the waterfall.

I shouted to him,

'Nate!' and he turned round and I saw that smile again like he'd given to Annabel the morning she called him Uncle Nathan and I smiled right back and thought I'd never been so happy before at all.

'I just kind of hid up here in the hills for a while, I didn't want to move away from the farm, I wanted to know how I could get back to the farm and to you, I wanted to stop here and find out why Ma hates me so.'

I wondered if I should tell Nate Ma didn't hate him none, I could feel her love for him like you can feel the rain in the air and see it in the heavy sky when it wants to come but can't, but I didn't want to talk then, I wanted Nate to go right on and tell me what he had to tell.

'But I been too long in jail, I got a gun but I forgot how to use it, it ain't like it was in the War where they give you a gun and tell you to lie in a ditch or run across a field and shoot at something in rags maybe used to be a man in a grey uniform, it ain't like that, and I couldn't kill enough to keep alive and when I killed I done it cruel, couldn't shoot well enough to do it clean, and then I couldn't keep a fire in to cook it, so I ended hungry and thought, well, I can't go straight back to the farm, need time to work out exactly what I am going to do, so I'd have to find work, leave the mountain. Don't get this wrong though, Sissy, I ain't being turned out of my own farm, but I got to think on it a while, no sense rushing in just to have that feller break my neck for me.'

I was relieved to hear Nate say that. I realised that all the time since he'd left I'd been waiting, tensed up like a coil, for him to come back and face Swann. Part of me wanted him to do it, as well, but like Nate hisself I knew that if he tried it now Swann would probably kill him.

I watched his face while I waited for him to go on. There were things in it I couldn't read, things buried deep behind his eyes. There seemed, out there in the forest, a moment of perfect silence, as if the world had ended and left us to ourselves, in peace. I closed my eyes and heard Nate's voice break through the sweet tranquillity of the place.

'So I set out one morning more'n a week ago and I walked all day,' Nate said, 'then I come to a place lower down the river and I saw a boy, no more'n fifteen, riding on a pony along the road there, and I said to him, Who owns this land around here? and he answers me, real polite and friendly, John Turner, sir, and I was mighty glad because I didn't recall his name, so I said, He from back east some place? and the boy said he didn't know but Mr Turner ain't been farming round here more'n three years.

'I asked him what had happened to all the folks used to farm around there, and he said Mr Turner had rightly owned all the land for miles around, it was a land grant he said, and so all the people who'd settled there had had to get off that land and most of them had headed up to Oregon. I guess our farm borders Turner land at that, because we don't seem to have no neighbours at all to the south of here. I was glad enough for that, didn't want none of those folks recognising me and making trouble.

'Now I had gotten real lucky here, because it turns out the boy works for this Mr Turner, they call him Pete Anderson, and cause he is only fifteen or so and hasn't got no folks, he's kind of a favourite of the Turners and knows everyone around there.

'So the boy showed me up to the house and I walked on up there, I saw Mr Turner hisself and I said, Sir, can you use a hand? and he said, looking me up and down, Can you work? so I said, Well, Mr Turner, I am hungry as a man can be but I was raised on a farm and if you will give me a dish of beans and some water to wash 'em down I will work as much as a man twice my size. So Mr Turner said he would try me out and if I could work he could use me and I would be picking up wages. I guess hands are pretty scarce out here still and Mr Turner's place been growing faster than he could keep up.

'So then, being as I could work and knew I could, I only had one problem, which was I knew you would be wondering about me and I wanted to see you again so bad. But that trading boat come round and Mr Packer, the one that runs that boat along the river here, he seemed like a man you could trust, so I got talking to him, he told me he would get a message to you, and I knew somehow I could trust him to do it.'

I asked Nate how he got over there and he said that the hands on the Turner place could always take a horse Saturday night and they went into town mostly, but he told them, and he blushed when he said this, which made me smile, told them he had a sweetheart lived on a farm he'd worked on for a little while, said he couldn't say nothing about having a sister or a Ma there because they might start asking questions and he didn't want Mr Turner to find out nothing about what had happened with him and Pa. Only Mr Packer knew we were brother and sister.

Nate said he rode that horse up to where the road ended then he had walked another three or maybe four miles along the riverbank where he didn't think the horse could get, but that next time we met he was going to ride the horse to the end of the road and then use a rowboat which a friend of his, the boy who had first directed him to the Turner place, was going to get for him and hide in the trees on the riverbank just where he had to leave his horse. That way he could carry on coming along the river, and not have to go round near to our farmhouse as he would if he rode across country.

I listened to all this, but really I was thinking about something else, and because I didn't want to be doing that, because I wanted to concentrate all the time on what Nate was saying to me and on the sound of his voice, I had to get this said, had to hear what he had to say, hear it so the trouble in my mind could be driven out.

So then I asked it, right out, me that's not used to saying nothing in case Swann takes it in his head I shouldn't, I asked Nate right out, because with Nate you felt straight away you could and had to ask things right out, what had happened with Pa, how Pa had ended dead and Nate had wound up in jail for it.

'Ain't Ma never told you nothing about that?'

I told him no, that Ma never talked about it, except she said him and Pa had an argument and there was a fight and it was kind of an accident that Pa wound up dead.

'She didn't blame neither of you for it,' was what I told Nate. Nate looked kind of impatient then, and he said,

'Ma wouldn't never say the truth about Pa, except when she was in that court and she had to say the truth to keep me from hanging.'

He was quiet for a while. It had grown pretty dark and I was starting to think I ought to be going back, though I wanted so much for Nate to say what he had to say.

But right then he stood up on the rock and said,

'I got to get back.'

There was no more talk that night, not about Pa, anyhow. Nate asked me about how I was and the children and Ma, but I didn't tell him. I didn't need to.

He knew.

3

Swann

Swann come by the farm the first time about five years before the day Nate come home from jail.

I was thirteen years old.

We done our best but the place was going down, there was only Ma and me. Most times we didn't have enough to eat, Ma never had enough, only in the real starving times did I go short while she went without. It was hard work even for a woman like Ma, with no-one but a little girl to help her.

None of the neighbours come round to help: because of what happened with Nate and Pa, we lost two men and couldn't get no others. Then when Turner arrived to claim his land everyone to the south of us was given three years to quit, and that caused a lot of resentment toward us. Ma was always scared something would happen, not that the neighbours would do anything to harm us but that they wouldn't do nothing to help us, neither. If trouble came, we'd have to face it alone.

We found Swann in the barn, about half dead from a bullet wound, he never told us how he got it, not that nor nothing else about his life before he come here. It was like he come out of Hell.

Ma knew how to take out the bullet from when she had

to do it on the trail West, there was some kind of trouble Ma wouldn't talk about, except she told me Pa's mother, who died before they reached California, she had shown her how to take out a bullet and Ma had done it more than once. It was a long time ago, but that didn't bother Ma, she was not a woman to forget.

Swann never spoke while Ma was nursing him, feeding him on our best, killing chickens we needed for eggs so's he'd have broth to make up his lost blood. It was near a week before he said a word. He just lay like an animal, watching us, first of all like he was afraid of us and then, when he started to get strong, looking to see what he could best use us for.

I was there the first time he spoke. He said,

'Your man don't mind this?'

Ma had to decide then. She could've said he was away, hoped Swann would believe her, made up some kind of story. It might not have worked, but it would've stopped Swann having any kind of claim on us. She didn't speak, carried on changing the dressing on his wound. I was stood behind her, in the light, over by the door of the barn. I could see Swann looking at me. Then Ma said,

'Ain't no menfolk here, mister.'

Swann said,

'How do you get along?'

'Me and Sissy here work all day and all night is how. When you're well enough to get on your feet and walk out and see the farm here, you will see how much good it does us.'

Swann never even asked what had become of the men. Ma told him maybe a year later about Nate and Pa, but he wasn't really interested.

It was planting time when she nursed him back to health, he just got up one morning and took the seed that was laying waiting to go in the ground, weren't but corn and beans and maybe a few potatoes and greens, and planted it out. He had money, too, and he went into town and come back the next day with a milk cow. We hadn't had no milk or butter or cheese at that time for three years, except what we might get from the trading boat. Our cows had all gone blind and dried up, and we didn't know what to do for them. Ma killed one and butchered it herself but the meat made us sick to the stomach and so we couldn't eat no more. We dried some of it and gave it to Pirate and he seemed able to stomach it but we never could. In the end Ma burnt all the carcasses in case we might get the disease ouselves. This left us with nothing but the chickens and what we could grow.

For a time Ma was for packing up and going some place, Sacramento maybe, to see if we couldn't find some kind of work. But we stuck it, and then the boatman gave her the idea of buying cloth and making it up into clothes to sell. She began to make all kinds of things, found she could sell shirts to the Indians, but found too she had a talent for making gloves which Mr Packer would buy back from her and sell up and down the river. I couldn't manage the gloves but I learnt to make money belts which we could sell to the boat.

Sometimes she would bake cookies but that didn't work out so well as neither me nor her could stop ourselves from eating up the profit. Then if the women on the other farms found out where the cookies come from they wouldn't buy them, in case they ate some of our luck, but I guess they thought the gloves and things were brought in from back east. Ma was a middling cook but a good seamstress, her stuff never did look homespun.

So Swann buying that fine cow he come back with that day, then a team of oxen to pull our wagon, these were no small things in our lives. He bought paint, too, and other things to do up the barn and the house. And though Ma knew he was finding an easy way to make a home for hisself, though she was aware that he was not an angel the Lord had sent to reward her virtue, she must have thought all this through and decided to let Swann move in like that. Like Ma said, he did enough work for three men and only ate enough for two.

He would sleep in the barn and hardly ever come in the house except for his meals. He never asked for nothing beyond his food, although I think it was understood that as long as he was working there the farm was part his, he wasn't working for no wages. He never did a thing, though, to make us feel any good toward him. He could see the hole we were in and must have known his work would be enough. I know now a man don't sweettalk a woman if he can just buy her, and hungry women come cheap.

I was too young to know better, but Ma was waiting and watching him. He aged her, like Nate and Pa aged her, but she wasn't so old then. Swann wasn't that much younger than her and she was expecting some night to find him in her bed. I could feel it in her, too, later when I was more growed, she hated Swann near as bad as I did but she was jealous as well, jealous he didn't choose her.

He come in one night later than usual from the field. He sat down, ate his plate of food, and told Ma to bring him some whisky. She put it down in front of him and he said,

'I'm sick of sleeping out there in the barn like a dog.'

Ma looked at him, smoothed down her apron, and said,

'We can bed you down in here, that ain't no problem.'

And Swann said,

'I need to bed down with a woman. I can get a whore in town but it ain't enough.'

Ma shot a look over at me and said,

'Don't talk that way in front of the child.'

36

Swann laughed, took a pull on his whisky, and looked round at me. His eyes kind of walked over my body. He said,

'I'm looking at her and I don't see no child. You think I meant I wanted to bed you?'

That anger come into Ma's eyes then and she looked over at me and almost shouted, as if it were me to blame,

'Sissy, go call Pirate home.'

I didn't need asking twice, but I stood outside the door a minute and I heard her raise her voice and Swann laughing in that mean way of his.

When I come back Swann got up and left. He didn't speak or even look at me. I heard Pirate bark at him like he always did, and Swann curse, then Pirate yelp when Swann kicked him. Swann put up with Pirate hating him for maybe six months then beat him so bad Ma had to shoot Pirate to put him out of his pain. I wished by then she'd do that for me as well.

Next morning he was gone before we got up, and he hadn't come back before dark. Three days went by like this and I was beginning to hope he had cleared out, leaving us richer by several head of cattle and a rebuilt barn. I knew though that those things were just what meant he would be back.

He rode in on the fourth day after his leaving, well before noon, and brought back a load of lumber which it turned out was payment for chopping some trees in the hills up to the north of here. That was all we could get out of him.

He used the wood to build a kitchen on the back of the cabin. He never asked us, to my knowledge, if that was what we wanted, but I knew that Ma had always wanted more space and that if she was to start making cheese and butter again then we were going to need it.

He dug out a cellar all by hisself and laid up the walls with rocks he carried down from the edge of the forest where you could find them strewn around, big hard rocks which didn't seem to have no place in that country. Swann would lay them one at a time on the ox wagon, the Lord knows how he got them on there but when he arrived with them outside the cabin he would grunt and heave and slide the big rock off the cart and then split it into long straight pieces, smooth as planed wood, which he carried round to where he'd dug the cellar, laying them up carefully against the new dug dirt to form the walls.

Ma stood and watched him, brought him coffee, made him huge stews of beans and chicken and salt beef she got from the boat. Sometimes he'd get the stew and pour sorghum all over it and push it into his mouth with big hunks of corn bread which would leave his beard and shirt covered in this sticky mess. I couldn't watch him eat, but Ma could. She watched him all day, followed his movements, fed him like she was fattening him for slaughter. There was something about her watching of him I didn't like, I had to turn my head away to avoid seeing the look on her face when I caught her watching him move, carry a stone weighed as much as either of us did, lift an axe high over his head.

All this time he never spoke again about wanting a woman. I didn't know much, but I wondered if she was already going out to him in the barn at night. I knew he wanted to sleep with a woman and had some vague notion what it was he wanted to do, but I didn't really know. I was scared by what he'd said about me, too. So I was glad he didn't say no more about it, guessed that either Ma was giving him whatever it was he wanted, or that he'd lost the argument with her and given up.

When he'd finished laying the stones he rode off in the cart one morning and came back at night with some heavy logs of cedar and pine which he put over the cellar as joists, resting the floor of the new kitchen on them. After that he built the walls and roof in no time, working as he always did, harder and faster as he came to see the end of his task. Then he fitted in the new stove, while Ma tacked up some coloured cloth to the bare walls to make it look more cheerful.

Swann had been with us less than two months. He had replaced our herd, rebuilt our barn, planted our fields, mended the house and built on a new kitchen and cellar. He bought Ma new equipment for her dairying and never took a thing out except his food. None of this made up at all for the fear he had brought into my life, worse than the fear of hunger or dispossession that I'd lived with since I'd been old enough to think. I didn't like the way he spoke to Ma or the way she let him, carrying on looking at him in that way. But all the time he never laid a hand on me, contenting hisself with looks I couldn't begin to understand but knew enough to fear, looks that rested long on my body and which he made no attempt to disguise, all the time knowing he could take me whenever he wanted me, that I was weak and without protection and he was strong without the restraint of society or any kind of inner goodness or doubt of hisself.

The morning after he finished building the cellar and kitchen when I went out to the barn to milk the cows Swann was waiting for me. I could see the evil in him as soon as he appeared, but he stayed out of the way until he could get hisself in between me and the door. He took hold of me and told me if I made a sound he'd kill me, then he raped me. I can remember, clear as a picture in my mind, the stink of him close to that first time, the way he pulled down the front of my dress to get a look at my breasts, the sound of him laughing at my shame and the slow, deliberate strength of his movements.

After that he used me whenever he had a mind, warning

me that if I said a word to Ma he would kill me and her too. He didn't just force hisself on me, he did crazy things just to frighten and humiliate me. He liked to make me stand naked in the cold barn, shivering while he sat and stared at me, not moving. If Ma wasn't around he'd make me take off all my clothes to serve him his food, displaying myself to him in dirty ways while he ate. He made me do awful things, too awful to recall, things he couldn't even get a whore to do for him.

I don't know if Ma knew a thing about it. She'd made her stand against him and then I think she kind of closed her mind to it. The choices she had to make were too awful. Even if she could've gotten rid of Swann, set the law on him or maybe shot him in the back if she had the chance, then we would've just been back where we begun, no man and not enough hands to work nor food to eat. I could see Ma and how she would look around the farm, see it how it was before Swann came and see in her mind how it would be again, the decay and the grinding work, the loss of another herd. So she didn't want to know how Swann was using me, and I was too scared and confused by it to tell her.

All the time I grieved for my luck at having lost my father and brother like that, and imagined Nate coming back, a grown man bigger than Swann and meaner when he needed to be, but gentle and kind when he didn't. Nate would run Swann off the farm and take it over, and we would all live as happily as could be.

When I was little Ma used to tell me stories she remembered her Pa telling her, fairy stories with witches and ghosts and goblins and handsome men rescuing pretty girls from dungeons or towers or dragons, and before Swann came I used to imagine a prince from one of Ma's stories would come and sometimes he would marry Ma and be like he was my Pa, sometimes I would see this in a dream and it would be Pa, like he never died, but more often it was a daydream I had that a man would come and marry Ma and look after us both, love us both I guess. When I got a little older I started to imagine him marrying me instead of Ma, but the rest of the daydream was just the same.

Once when I was maybe ten the boatman left some packages behind on our landing by mistake, and I ran down the riverbank with some of them, yelling to him until he realised what he'd done and put back toward the bank to pick them up. I guess the packages must have been pretty important because he gave me some candy and a loaf of wheat bread, something I didn't remember tasting before, then he asked me if there was any little thing I wanted because I had just saved him some money and deserved a reward that I could keep to remind me that good turns always come back to you and that honesty was always the best policy, that we were put on God's world to help each other. Mr Packer liked to talk that way.

I knew Ma wanted a looking glass, that something, I don't remember what, had become of the one looking glass she had had, so I asked him if he had one. His wife went inside where the stocks were kept and brought out a little round glass with a wooden handle painted turquoise. I thought it was the most beautiful thing I'd ever seen.

I told Mrs Packer I was going to give the glass to Ma, although I knew we would both be able to use it. And she told me this, that before I gave that glass to my Ma I could use it to find out who I would marry when I was a growed up lady and lived in a fine big farm house with servants and a hundred horses.

All I had to do was to sit on the edge of a trough or rain barrel in the yard, hold the looking glass behind me so that the reflection of the water appeared in it, then look over my shoulder at it and I would see my future husband. But when I got back to the house, all excited to try it, running straight to the water trough and perching on the edge, I couldn't see nothing at all in the mirrored water. I decided the water in the yard trough was too muddy and murky to yield up any secrets and that I would have to find some that was clear and clean. But then the looking glass slipped from my hand and fell into the trough. I tried to fish it out, but the trough was deep and felt cold and somehow frightening, as if it might rise up and pull me down into itself. I started to sob and cry and Ma heard me and came out to me, scolding me for messing in the mud and dirtying my dress until I told her what had happened and she fished out the looking glass and rinsed it down and said how beautiful it was, carrying me into the house to get cleaned up and dry and all the time kissing me and hugging me tight.

I told Ma about the packages and gave her the bread and some of the candy I'd saved for her, but I didn't tell her about the game that Mrs Packer had told me how to play, nor how the looking glass had ended up in the trough. I never did try it again, neither, dropping it in the muddy water like that scared me from the game.

The harvest came in from fields grown heavy, fertilised with the sweat of Swann's back and gathered in by all of us, hands busy laying up the stores for winter. But there never was a harvest time with less joy in it, not one where the fields were so plump with ripe corn and the beans and vegetables so rich and plentiful.

It got so that any time Ma turned her back Swann would drag me out to the barn and make me do any dirty thing came into his head. I had nightmares about him, still do sometimes, and can't be sure any more what really happened and what I dreamed. I know he would gag me to stop Ma hearing me screaming, and hold a cigar close to my skin so that I could feel the heat of it. But I don't know if he ever let it touch. He had other ways to hurt me would leave no mark for Ma to see, or maybe he was afraid I would show the boatman or his wife.

All the torments he put me through made me feel more helpless and lonely and afraid. I dreamed of Nate as my protector, or that the ghost of Pa would come one night to strike him down. And all the time Ma, who hardly left the house before Swann came, seemed to find more reasons to go out to the field or down to the river and the forest, walking out into the winter, leaving me at his mercy. Oh, she didn't know the terrible suffering he put me through, but she must have suspected him at least of using me for his whore.

It wasn't me told her, wasn't me made it so she couldn't pretend she didn't know no more, it was Annabel. Ma knew I was with child fore I did, and I think Swann knew before either of us, because he must've noticed I missed the curse and Ma didn't know nothing till I started to show and I didn't know till I heard her raising her voice again at him.

I come into the room, he was setting at the table with his whisky and Ma took me in her arms and started to cry. I asked her what was ailing her, but she just cried and cried. Then Swann said,

'You ain't got no more sense than a skunk, less, cause a skunk knows when it is pregnant I guess.' And he laughed.

Ma turned to him and let go of me and kind of hissed, like an angry cat, told Swann to get out, pack up his things and don't come back.

He laughed again, and said,

'First, it'll soon be planting time again and you ain't gonna get enough in the ground without me. Second, I ain't leaving all the work I've done here and the herd and all and just riding off with a thank you ma'am. Third, you soon gonna have another mouth to feed and you is gonna be in shit without me to do it for you. So why don't you just shut up and get me something to eat?'

I was scared, like I always was when Swann was around, and scared too because I knew something was going on in my body and I thought I was real ill and would soon die. I looked at Ma and asked her if Swann and her meant she was going to have another baby. She looked back at me, like she was going to cry again, and Swann roared with laughter.

Ma didn't cry, she just said,

'I'm awful sorry, Sissy.'

Then Swann got up, walked into her room, came out again and said,

'Your bed's bigger'n hern, so you can have hers and we'll have yours.'

Ma walked over to the stove and poured some beans over a slice of fat bacon. She put the plate on the table and walked back over to me. She said,

'You know the dirty things Swann has been doing to you?'

I wondered how she knew, but I just hung my head, shamed, and nodded a little. Swann roared out laughing again but this time Ma turned to him and shouted,

'You shut up, you hear, shut up and eat or I swear you will have to kill me.'

Swann grinned, but he didn't laugh no more nor answer Ma back, he ate up his beans and bacon without another word. He even got up to fill his whisky jug hisself.

Ma said,

'Well, Sissy, he has put his seed inside of you when he done that. You will be having a baby in maybe five months, maybe a little longer, and Swann will be its pa.

So things will only be decent now if he takes you for his wife.'

And that was how it was, Ma was the only thing I had for a preacher like she would be the only one I had for a midwife, but as I didn't expect nothing but misery by that time I just took it, and Swann moved into the house and took me to bed and used me most every night, even when I was with child.

4

Summer, 1866

When I went to leave the house the next Saturday night Ma said,

'You're going to meet Nathan, ain't you?'

I didn't speak to her, I just stood like I stood and felt like I felt when she asked about me and Swann. She said,

'He working near here?'

I still didn't answer.

Then she said,

'You know what Swann will do to you and him if he finds out you're meeting?'

I swallowed, cause my throat was dry and I felt hot inside myself, in my belly and head and hands, and I nodded just enough for Ma to see. Then, I didn't look at her at all, but I had to speak, had to tell her, and I said,

'Ma, Nate is my brother and he is kind to me.' Then I picked up my gun and went out before she had time to answer.

When I walked through the wood to meet him I felt like I was going to cry. I could see and feel it now inside Ma that she hated Nate, even though she was his Ma and I could feel she still loved him, too. I have never felt so much pain in anything like I felt in Ma when she spoke about Nate, and sometimes too when she was sitting by the stove, staring ahead of her at something, not speaking at all. If I thought real hard on Ma when she was doing that I could see what she saw, which was faces, her face and mine, and a little girl's face I could feel was me, and my babies' faces and then Nate's face and the face of Nate much younger and then a face I could hardly remember, Pa's face, then all the faces would spin like the colours on the boatman's toy, spin and spin till the colours disappeared and there weren't nothing but a hole, a blur where the colours had been, sometimes white like the toy and sometimes black like a moonless night, and then there would be Swann's face, in the whiteness or blackness, blizzard or storm, Swann's face like the trouble in the air they used to see sometimes on the trail and that Ma calls a dust devil, Swann's face laughing like he did when I was with child and too much a child myself to know, Swann's face with his mouth open crying out and sweat on his brow and eyes shining bright in his head like when he would use me and finish it and he would jerk like a chicken when you wring her neck and cry out his hard deep man's cries and the seed come from him that was worse in the fear it gave than the pain or his hate of me.

And I could see all these things in Ma's silence. And I ain't never felt nothing like I felt and saw in Ma unless it was the bewildered love and pain and fear when I held Pirate and his blood covered my dress and I held him and cried just before Ma had to shoot him.

So when I got to Nate he could see the tears inside my face and I couldn't help but ask him, I had to know there and right away, before I could sit with him on the riverbank and feel my love for him and his for me, so I said, before he could speak,

'Nate, tell me how come you killed Pa.'

And then the tears come out of my face and I had to sit down on the bank among the rocks and Nate held on to me and I was glad of the warmth of his body but I couldn't feel no warmth of love, not until he had told me, and I had to stop the tears so's he could speak and I could listen on his words. Nate said,

'Sissy, why you crying, what's been said to you make you cry and asking about me'n Pa like that fore I can even say hello to you?' And he sounded kind of scared.

But I didn't want none of that and I had to make myself strong and say to him,

'Please, Nate, I have to know what it was like, he was my Pa and your Pa and if you hadn't done that maybe things wouldn't've been like this for any of us with Pa not dead and you not in jail all that time, and me and Ma . . . ' but I didn't want to say nothing about that because I knew Nate couldn't do a thing about any of it, so I shut up and just looked at him, told him with my mind I wanted him to speak, I needed to know.

Then Nate had to ask me if Swann ever beat me, and I could feel an anger in me like I see in Ma but ain't used to seeing it in myself, and I said,

'Nate, I don't want to talk none about Swann and me, least not tonight, fore I can talk about anything, I have to know about you and Pa.'

But Nate said,

'It has to do with me and Pa,' and I knew he was telling true. So I said, real low, like in a whisper,

'Swann beats me sometimes, yes, but if you come and try to stop him he'll kill you and I would rather have the beating than you dead, and anyhow after he got through killing you he would go right on beating me.'

And Nate put his arm round me again, just his arm round my shoulder this time while we were sitting there, it was maybe July now and real warm, darkness just coming on, and I leant against him and for a moment I didn't care no

more how he had killed Pa. Then I thought of the faces Ma
had to see and I said,

'Tell me, Nate, please tell me now.'

He let go of me and stood up, stood with his back against
a rock, facing me, and he said,

'I only asked if Swann beat you because if he did that
would be the same. I put up with Pa's beatings for sixteen
years. Any time I didn't please him he would whip me with
a strap, take a stick to me, or just use his hands on me. I
was scared to look on my own Pa's hands. I couldn't never
please him.'

I could hear a shivering in Nate's throat like he was going
to cry, but he didn't, he was quiet for a little while then he
kept right on.

'When I was very small there were some women lived
not five miles from here who decided they would start up a
school. They hired a teacher and everything. I hated to go to
that school and he beat me for not going when I should've.
Then they got a different teacher and I got to like it, got to
want to be there, and he beat me cause I wanted to go when
he needed me to help around the farm. He beat me every
time I made any kind of mistake, like the things kids do,
and he didn't beat me like a father but as if he hated me. It
was the hate, Sissy, it weren't the beating, it was the way I
couldn't never please him and the hate I could feel when he
looked at me.'

It was almost full dark, now, and I couldn't see Nate's
face no more, but I could see inside him, a great pain as big
and as hard as Ma's pain, a bewilderment like Pirate's when
he was dying there in my arms.

'I was sixteen,' Nate said then, 'when Pa hit me for the
first time with his fist, he made my nose bleed and my head
go kind of foggy and I ain't never been so scared. I waited
till the bleeding stopped then I went into the room where my

bed and things were. I had a little money I'd earned from writing, I used to write letters and things for folks around here and they would pay me. I had more'n three dollars and I figured it would feed me till I could find work. I wanted to work on a newspaper, not writing it but helping to set the type, like I'd seen boys doing one time when Pa took me to Chico. Pa said always he needed me on the farm, and it was true, I knew it, so I'd pretty well give up the idea. But now I thought if he was going to start hitting me with his fists, a man that was twice my size or more, and still looked to me like a giant, I couldn't be expected to put up with no more.

'I thought maybe I could go off to Sacramento or down further into Southern California and look for work. So I got my things and my money and I was going to leave while he was out to the field, cause I knew he wouldn't stand around waiting to wish me farewell. But when I come out of my room, the room where both us kids slept then, he was standing there, he'd come back from the field and I still don't know why he done that. Ma was over by the window, sewing or darning something I think. I come out and I didn't say a word to either of them and I was standing by the stove, warming myself before I set off, cause it was still early in the year and cold, though the worst of the winter had passed. Then it just happened, Sissy, it just happened.'

I could barely make out Nathan's form in the darkness, bowed a little like he was carrying something. Then I saw him move and hunker down, bringing his face much closer to mine, leaning forward like he was still trying to look at me, even though there was no moon and near no light at all. He was quiet a long time until I said,

'Tell me, Nate.'

And it was like he was still not wanting to tell me all of it, he wanted to leave it there and let me figure the rest out. I could see him a little better now, the sky was full of stars and the starlight seemed to reflect in the water, lighting Nate's face so dimly it was hard to tell if my mind was putting the shape of his face there before and above me in the pitch blackness, but lighting it from below, from the starlight on the river.

Nate said,

'Don't you have to go yet, Sissy? I don't know if I can say any more. He come at me then and I hit him, cause I was scared and defending myself from him, and I still don't know if I could've done different.'

I said,

'You have to tell me, Nate, you have to tell me, and I don't need to go nowhere, because Ma already knows I'm meeting you out here and Swann don't never come back until it's light.'

But Nate kept on. He tried to say Ma might be worried if I was too late, that the babies might wake and be scared because I wasn't there. I felt my anger again, like Ma's anger. I thought I would cry but didn't. I said,

'Nate, I don't care if Ma is worried. I don't even care if for one time in his life Swann comes back and he kills me when I get home. I ain't never asked nobody for nothing but I am asking you, now, to tell me how you killed Pa.'

Nate was quiet. I thought he was holding his face in his hands, but I knew he wasn't crying tears. Then he said,

'Pa told me I wasn't going nowhere. He said he needed me round the farm, that it was my place as his son to work the farm with him. I told him I would stay if he stopped beating me. He swore at me, said if I didn't work I had to expect a beating, said as long as he was alive and could work I would have to do as he said. I told him I would do as he said like decent people, in the way decent and free working men done like they was told by whoever was paying their wages and if they didn't like it they could go someplace else.

Said I heard it told around that a lot of men had started to think that even niggers should be free enough for that.

'Pa said I shouldn't tell him nothing about politics until I was at least old enough to vote, he said, Don't you tell me what you learned in your fancy schoolbooks and your crazy abolitionist newspapers about that. I could see he was blind mad with me, I didn't know why, but I tried to calm him and I said, All I'm saying Pa – I was going to say I was only asking to be treated like a human being, but he wouldn't let me go on, he wouldn't never let me say my piece, Sissy.'

He stopped for a moment, waited like he was expecting me to say something to him, but I could feel he wasn't going to stop now, that he was going to tell me at last what no-one ever would.

'He come right up to me and he said, You are my son and I will treat with you just how I see fit. I was backed up against the stove. I could feel it burning my back and legs. He was leaning over me. If I'd let it go at that it would've been the finish of me, Sissy. He was saying I had no more rights than a slave. I said, and I wish I'd said it different, some way that would've made him less mad, the only thing I really feel guilt for is I know I said it to make him just as mad as I could, I don't know why but I wanted him mad at me, wanted this to be the last fight we would have, didn't want, I guess, to be a child no more, felt myself a man with rights like him, I said, You saying, Pa, that Mr Fremont would likely make a man free if he's a nigger but not if he's your son?

'And Pa lifted his fist like I knew he would, I guess, and I reached down and picked up the fire-iron that was the only thing I could reach, and before he could hit me I swung it round and just before I hit him I saw Ma behind him, heard her scream and cry out, but I brought that iron round on to the side of Pa's head and saw him go down on to his knees,

52

his hand on the side of his head there, blood on his head. And I walked round him and Ma, threw the iron over to the other side of the room, and walked over to the door.

'I turned round to tell Ma I was going, just because I didn't want to leave without another word, I knew I was going to have to go where Pa couldn't find me and I might not see her again, so I turned round just to say, I don't know, that I was sorry it had all come out this way. And then I saw Pa, lying out on the ground, the blood coming from the side of his head, and Ma let out another awful scream and went to him, she took him in her arms and his body started to twitch and shake and blood come out his mouth and then he was still.

'I went over to him and I said, well I cussed I guess, but Ma acted like she didn't know I was there, she just held his head in her arms, the blood pouring on to her hands and clothes, and she rocked back and forward and cried and cried with a sound I ain't heard before or since, like it didn't come from this world at all. I knew Pa was dead, knew there wasn't nothing anybody could do. I took a horse and first I rode over to Doc Saunders and told him Pa had fallen and cracked his head and was bleeding bad from it, so the Doc would ride over fast. Then I told him some story about someone else who needed to know and I went on into town and told the Sheriff what had happened and they locked me up and there was the trial and all and they took what I said, and Ma backed me up about how he had treated me, but they didn't pay her no heed, they didn't want nobody killed his own Pa to live, so they told me they was going to put a rope around my neck and that would be the end of my sixteen years, yes.'

It was like now Nate had told me he wanted to go on talking to soothe it some, but I'd heard what I wanted to hear and, now I knew, I wanted to get back to Ma, didn't want to leave her alone in that room with the faces spinning in front of her, though I knew Nate needed me too, that he had his faces and his spinning colours and moonless nights and blizzards that froze the soul, and I could feel and see when I looked into him, past the black nights and white storms of ice he had to live inside, that he was telling me true, that Pa had hated him and driven him, that he hadn't given him no love nor any of hisself, and that he had done what I would have to do to Swann, if I was going to save my babies from him.

5

Elizabeth, Elizabeth

Nate taught me to read.

He would write the letters on a little piece of slate he got from Mr Turner's children. He taught me new letters every week and how to put them together into words. I learned fast, and by the time the first snows come to the valley I could read a whole lot, though nowhere near as good as Nate. He would read books with hardly any pictures to help you along, books with real stories about men and women, rich ones and poor, and the lives they lived far from here in big cities and places where it was hot all the time. But the books I could read were meant for little children. I picked up the reading fast because I'd been wanting to learn it for so long.

I carried on meeting Nate every Saturday night until late in the fall.

These were the best of times we had together, before anything come between us, when I felt us locked tight together in the knowledge of each other's suffering and fear. Even though Nate had turned out to be a man much smaller than Swann, and near as fearful of his hand as I was, I still felt with all my heart that he would rescue me, that the dreams I'd had of him would come back as blessings and that life, my life, could still make good the promises it had always, in spite of everything, whispered in my ear.

Whatever doubts I may have felt in Nate were forgotten whenever we met. I never knew, from one time to the next, from one moment to the next, whether his mood would lead us to horseplay or to the terrible falling sorrow that would sometimes come over him, when all I could do was to comfort him, holding him and chasing demons from him, even as I might do for Annabel. Other times he would tell me things that had happened to him in prison or in the army, friends he'd had or bullies he'd lived in fear of, then the stories would take him up or down, to happiness or despair, as the memories came to him.

A few names came again and again. For a year in prison a man named Mandel had pursued him, terrified him, forced him to act as his servant, stole from him the precious few consolations of his awful life.

'I remember when Mandel first arrived, they put him in a cell with five others of us, I'd been there around a year,' Nate told me. I remember the first time he told me about Mandel, we were sitting in the darkness, well into the fall, close together for warmth, and I felt him shudder when he spoke of him. Whenever Nate mentioned Mandel it seemed to be cold and dark, as if the warmth and daylight banished him, or drove him back into that cell in Nate's mind.

'He had been beaten bad by somebody, maybe guards at the jail where he'd been before, waiting for his trial, and he didn't say or do nothing for a week. But all the time I knew he was watching me, and I could feel the others in the cell waiting for something to happen.'

Nate went off into a silence when he'd told me that. I waited, but nothing came.

'Then did he hurt you, Nate?' I asked him, and felt

his body brace at the thoughts the question brought into his mind.

'He kept it going for a whole year,' he said at last. 'He made me do his chores, mend his clothes, things like that. He would do things like, well, he would take my wrist and squeeze it, or drag me across the cell by my hair. He was a big man, and I was just a boy.'

'Didn't the others ever help you, or try to?' I said, angry with these unknown men who'd left my brother to suffer alone.

He didn't answer for a while. Then he said,

'They were part of it, Sissy, they liked to watch him hurting me, they'd laugh at me, even sometimes join in if he'd let them.'

'Did he hurt you bad?'

I remember asking him that and feeling him start like he could feel all the pain again. Without answering, he pulled away from me and told me he'd have to leave. He stood up and I followed him up the slope away from the river. He kissed me like he always did, soft as down on my upturned cheek, just below my eye, as if he were always kissing away tears he feared would be there.

'Yes, Sissy,' he said, 'he hurt me bad. If I told you the things he done to me, the way the others would urge him on to it, you'd have to feel the pain of it too. It won't leave me, Sissy, it won't never leave me. But now I got you to help me along,' and his voice changed to the one he always used to tell his tall stories, 'so things ain't so bad.' And he squeezed my hand.

This was just like Nate. If a story got so that it had too much hurt in it for him, he'd sometimes go down into dark silence, down into his falling, but just as often he'd suddenly pull hisself out of it, try to make it sound like the awful things he'd suffered were nothing to him now. And it was true that sometimes, most of the time, Nate seemed light of heart. He was out of prison and knew there was no need for him ever to go back. He had survived four years of war, come home to a sister who loved him. He had a job, friends, and a way of understanding things that I knew would take him wherever he wanted to go. But then the other side would show itself to him, blocking out the light. There was Ma. There was the farm. There was my suffering and the frustration and helplessness he felt in the face of it.

We sustained each other, and I tried to make him see that, to keep his mind on that. I never had a moment's shyness with Nate, he came ready made as the friend I'd never had. I loved him with my blood before I did with my heart or mind, and he needed me so bad, so openly, that I had to give back to him even more than I took.

The giving was easy, though; I knew about that, as any mother must. The only pain I had from it was when he would not let me give. There was always that secret place locked inside him, the stories unfinished as the pain became too great, the sudden change of mood that did not stop me from feeling that he was falling, falling all the time toward some interior fate that waited him, impassive and indifferent as the surface of the water at the bottom of a well.

When I think about the girl I was, how few words I had then to say what I felt, I feel some great warmth of gratitude to Nate even now, or if not to Nate then to the Providence that brought him to me, that gave him time to teach me how to read, how to learn, how to reach out beyond the walls of my own prison and touch the blue sky. Nate and me, we were bound by sadness, we both skirted its shallow banks and sometimes ran aground on it, but we did not meet in gloom or despair, the sound of laughter punctuated our talk much more than did the sound of tears or anger at the world that had used us so. And it was the laughter that brought me to him, that seemed to bound a special place that was all our own, rescuing us from confusion and loneliness.

Everything made Nate laugh. He would watch ducks upending to feed and shout,

'And the same to you, ma'am!' in one of his voices. He liked to talk politics, but to Nate it wasn't the serious, long-faced business it seems to be to most, he would tell some tale of hypocrisy, of men disguising their greed behind fine words, and laugh at it all. Oh, I remember the troubles we had and the ones that were coming, but most of all I remember now the way Nate taught me the world, not just to read and write but to laugh, too, that's maybe served me just as much as all my books.

In the winter Swann would go off to town on Saturday as usual, only he would go earlier before dark fell and sometimes not come back till it was almost dark Sunday. I hoped that as the weather grew cold Nate could come to the house instead of us having to set freezing our bones down by the river. Swann would never know the difference. But when I asked Ma she shook her head. She said,

'If you want to go out to meet him that's your affair, ain't nobody got the right to stop you from seeing your own brother. But Swann don't care nothing for rights, least of all yourn, and if he ever finds out about it he'll kill him and likely you too.'

'How'll he find out?' I asked her, but just then James came toddling in and I had my answer. Ma glanced down at him and Annabel, who'd come chasing after him, and shook her head. James started to bang with a wooden spoon on an old bucket I'd given them to play with, and I had to raise my voice to make her hear me.

'We could fix something, Ma,' I said, and she couldn't

say it wasn't so, she had to come right out and say what was really on her mind.

'I don't want Nathan in this house again,' she said. 'That's all there is to it.' And she turned and snatched the spoon from James, making him look up bewildered at her, then start to cry.

'It's his house as well as ours, Ma,' I said to her, lifting James and holding him to me, but she clenched her fists and looked at me like she would hit me, which she never had done. She said,

'Like I told him, you don't come by a house by killing the man who owns it, nor a farm neither, even if the man is your own Pa. No.'

And I said,

'But Ma, Nate told me how come he killed Pa, and it wasn't hardly more'n an accident. He paid years of hard labour for doing that, then spent four years fighting for his country, but now you're making him pay worse than any judge. What you're doing to him is worse even than the rope that trial judge had waiting for him.'

James had stopped crying as sudden as he'd started, and was now wriggling to be put down. I lowered him to the floor, and watched him go straight for the spoon where Ma had put it down on the edge of the table.

'Nate needs us, Ma,' I said to her. It scared me to say so much and to go against Ma in that way, but there weren't nothing else I could do.

Ma stopped looking so mad, she looked at me like I was a little child, the way she did when she told me I was going to bear Annabel that time, and she shook her head and said,

'Nate didn't tell you true, Sissy, he told you the same as he told the judge and jury, the same story he had me tell to the governor to stop them from hanging him, the same I guess as he's told hisself all these years, just so's he could

60

live, and so's he could live with what he'd done, but there weren't no more truth in it then than there is now.'

'Ma, Nate told me what happened between him and Pa, how Pa died, he didn't want to tell me but I made him, and I knew when he told me that he was telling me true.'

'Then, Sissy,' Ma said, real quiet but with that anger she had inside her right there, close up, I could see it as plain as I could see her face, 'if you think what Nathan says about that is true you have to call your own Ma a liar, because I am telling you that everything Nate said at his trial, and I know he's still saying the same now as then, everything he said, or near everything, was a damned lie. And when Nate goes to Hell as he surely will, it won't be because he killed his Pa, but because he chose not to repent of it, chose instead to blacken his father's name in front of the world, and mine too if it come to that. And that is why I don't want him in my house no more, son as he is, why I would sooner be holden to Swann, that is no better'n an animal but no worse neither.'

James had started to bang on the pan again, but neither of us paid it no mind, and now he must have felt something, too, because he quit his noise and looked up, curious, at his Ma and Grandma raising their voices to each other. You could see he was thinking about crying, but didn't, just carried on staring in that way he had.

Ma walked away from me, over to her chair by the stove there, and she let herself down into it and stared straight ahead of her, not looking at me nor James nor any other thing of this world, but at something hanging in the air before her, something hidden from me that I couldn't see nor feel, something sat behind a veil of pain and tears that I nor any other never saw Ma shed, tears she must've shed alone at night in her bed, cold without Pa and with her boy far away in a prison she thought he'd built hisself. And I hadn't never, up to then, seen her look so old.

I couldn't let her, though, I couldn't let her be like that. I said,

'But Ma, Nathan said you backed him up at the trial, you told the judge everything he said was true.'

And Ma said,

'Sure I did. I was lying.'

Then she went quiet again, watching that hidden thing in front of her. James lost interest, toddled off to find Annabel. After a while Ma turned toward me and said,

'You expect me to let my own boy hang?'

'What you're doing now's worse than hanging, Ma,' I told her again. I scared myself saying that. It was as if someone else was talking with my voice. Ma looked at me, stared right through me almost deeper inside than I could see myself, and said,

'Sissy, do you know what it was like for me in that coutroom, telling those lies about your Pa? Maybe if you ever love a man—' She looked away for a moment, and I saw her swallow hard. When she turned back to me her face was like a blade, and she said,

'Can you imagine what I felt like, going to see the governor in my best dress that was about as good a garment as his serving girls would throw out, acting dumb like a good farm wife should, saying, Please Mister and Please Sir and begging him to commute Nate's sentence, repeating those lies about how Pa would beat him for nothing and had always hated him and never treated him like a father should? I done all that, and I done it only because I knew your Pa would have done anything to save his boy's neck, even after Nate knocked him to the ground like a mad dog, even though it meant telling the world a lie, a terrible lie, Sissy, that he wasn't a good man at all. But as bad a man as could be.'

She stopped and looked up toward the ceiling, then screwed her eyes up tight and slowly shook her head.

'Oh, Sissy,' she said, 'I wish you would let Nate be, tell him to get on up to Oregon and find hisself a parcel of land, take a woman up with him there to be his wife, forget about us, make some kind of life for hisself, do some good to balance all that bad he done. If you keep on seeing him, no good can come of it.'

I thought about what she said, and I tried to look into her to see why she was saying it, but I couldn't see nothing except a dark downward thing, like the well I saw Nate falling through the day he come home, but Ma wasn't falling, she wasn't anywhere in that darkness, or if she was anywhere she was down at the bottom, looking up and up to nothing but blackness and more blackness, nothing at all but that.

I didn't see as much of Nate during the winter. He was Mr Turner's most trusted hired man now, he told me, and the boatman said too he was getting along fine, so Mr Turner would send him off on errands down to Sacramento or even further, and he might be gone two or three weeks. He couldn't always let me know the week before if he was going to be there, so unless the weather was so bad I could tell he wouldn't be able to row upriver, I'd go down to the riverbank and wait.

Sometimes it was bitter cold and if Nate came we would wrap ourselves together in a blanket and sit in the shelter of some rocks to keep off the icy wind.

All winter I had tried to keep up my reading, reading the little book Nate had given me that I'd hidden behind the stove and could only take out for a few minutes at a time when Swann was out to the field or to town and Ma wasn't around and the children were asleep or playing in the yard. Swann would've beat me sore if he'd seen me reading, even if I could've convinced him that the book had come from some place, maybe from the trading boat, didn't involve Nate.

Ma sometimes blamed the fact that Nate could read for what he did to Pa. If the children, especially Annabel, had seen something pretty like my little picture book they would've wanted to play with it, would've said something about it to their Grandma, or even in front of Swann. So only when I was really on my own, maybe once in a week, could I get that little book out from behind the stove and look at it, read the words and fit them to the pictures, try to remember the sound every letter made in 'dog' and 'cat' and 'pin' and all the other forty or fifty words in there. I tried to do it like Nate said, not just to learn the words but to try and put the letters together into new words.

By spring I could read pretty good, because even though I couldn't get that book out so often, I could remember the shapes of the letters and make them up inside my head and look at them in the air in front of me. It was the only thing I had was all mine, and I loved it somehow like I loved Annabel and James and Nate and Ma. It made me feel hot and full when I thought of my book, feel things stronger than the fear I felt when I thought what would happen if Swann found out about it.

I hadn't seen Nate in over a month, but I knew he would be waiting for me that first Saturday night after the last snow thawed. Thaw started Tuesday, late in February or early March I guess it was, so I had the rest of the week to prepare for seeing him.

In the morning when I cleaned out the stove I took a piece of wood weren't burned right through, and I hid it in the chicken house. Then, when I got the chance, I brought that wood in, and I took out my book, I turned to the back where there was a page didn't have no words on it, and I put my own word there, I put it there with that piece of burned wood, I wrote 'sisi', and I looked at it writ there, and I liked it so much I wrote it right down there again, 'sisi', my own word and my own name that nobody ever showed me how to write, but that I knew the 's' from 'sun' and the 'i' from 'pin' and I thought if I put them together like that, and done it twice, it would come out just about right.

Then I hid my book and sat by the stove, happier I think than I had ever been, happier even than when I was playing there with my babies and Swann wasn't here, happier than when I was with Nate. And I wasn't just happy because I done that, because I wrote down how I thought you wrote Sissy, but because I knew that if Swann didn't find what I was doing and kill me for it, then by the time harvest was in and the snows come again, I'd be able to get a piece of burned wood, or maybe buy a pencil from the boatman, and if I had a piece of paper I'd be able to sit right here and write it all, write my given name full and proud,

Elizabeth, Elizabeth.

6

Spring, 1867

I was getting ready to go meet Nate, it was about four weeks after the snows thawed, coming warm out of spring, and Ma said,

'Don't go tonight, Sissy.'

I didn't even look at her, I could feel it in her every time since winter I'd been to meet him that she didn't want me to go, so I'd been waiting for her to speak out. I said,

'I have to go, Ma, Nate will be waiting for me. If I don't go he won't know what has happened, he'll worry, he might even come down here, which you said you didn't want him to do.'

'If you go on seeing him he'll come on down here some time anyway, he'll come back for what he thinks is his, and Swann will kill him.'

'This is his home, Ma,' I told her.

I was pinning up my hair and spoke through a mouthful of pins, looking at myself in that same looking glass that had refused to show me who I would marry, waiting for her to get mad again; but she didn't get angry like she had before when Nate said the farm was his, she just sounded tired now, awful tired.

'Swann don't care whose farm you say it is or Nate says or me or the State of California. If he finds out you are meeting Nate, or if Nate comes down here, he'll kill him. You think you can go on meeting him down there on the river every Saturday night and Swann ain't going to know?'

I said,

'Ma, Swann ain't God or even Satan, we can beat him, we can get the farm back for us and Nate.'

I said all that, though I didn't know how I could make it come true.

Ma looked at me again like I was a child, full of crazy dreams, and I wondered if Pa used to look at Nate that way when he talked about the things he learned from school. I still couldn't read grown ups' books real well but Nate would always read to me when we met, and I knew there was something out beyond this piece of ground where Swann kept us all like cattle.

Ma carried on looking at me and then shook her head.

'I told you, Sissy, I don't want Nate here any more'n Swann does.'

I asked her why. She didn't speak for a while, and I was thinking of leaving her to it. Then she said,

'Because Nate lied to you, like I already told you. He stood up in court and lied. He told the judge Pa had beaten him bad all his life, like I had just stood by and let him. I do my best to keep Swann from hitting you, Sissy, and you know it.'

I nodded to her, because it was true. Ma could stand up to Swann like I never could, but she would only do it if she thought Swann would hurt me real bad. The slaps he gave me whenever I didn't please him she didn't pay much mind.

'So I had to stand up in court and say, Sure, Nathan's father always did hate him, he made his life Hell, he was mean to him and beat up on him all the time. And so I had to blacken your Pa's name, that was dead and couldn't speak up for hisself, and I had to act like I was too weak or too feared myself to protect my own son from this unnatural father hated the flesh of his flesh, I had to do all that to keep Nathan from the gallows he deserved. And when I'd done it all once in court in front of all those people, people who were neighbours and had been friends to us, then I had to do it all again in front of the governor, who looked at me all the time I was talking like I was a crazy woman, like it should've been me they was hanging for letting all of this happen in my home.'

Ma cried. She cried long and hard, she didn't attempt to hold her tears back, she cried like that for the first time as far as I could remember, though I knew she only saved her tears for when she was alone. I understood now, that it wasn't Pa's reputation she had been ashamed to blacken, but her own, and that it wasn't really anyone else's view of her she cared for, but her own feelings about herself. She had seen herself as a good woman and a good mother, and what Nate had told the court and me, what the court and me had both believed, made it impossible to go on seeing herself that way.

I put my hands on her shoulders and tried to turn her to take her in my arms and hold her safe from the cold at the bottom of that deep dark well I could feel around her, hold her from its blackness and fear, but she wouldn't be turned. I couldn't leave and couldn't stay. Nate had his story and Ma had hers, and when I looked into either of them all I could see was truth and righteousness and passion, that each thought the other had done them wrong, that they were saying things they knew were true.

How could I know what took place when Nate killed Pa? I had lived near eight years when it happened. I knew Pa never laid a finger on me and I didn't remember him beating

Nate, but that don't mean it never was. Ma looked up at me after a while and she said,

'You'd better be going if you want to see Nate.'

I said, quiet,

'It's all right, Ma, Nate knows it's hard for me to get away. He'll wait all night if he has to.'

I held on to her shoulders, but she still wouldn't turn to let me hold her like I wanted. She said,

'Sissy, I want you to know how it really happened.'

It felt like she was holding on to herself, like you do on a hillside in winter when you're scared you'll slip. She wanted me to go, now, so she could cry again on her own, cry for Pa and all the rest of us, but mostly for him, cry because his arms weren't there no more, to turn her and hold her away from that darkness I could see around her.

'Your Pa never hit Nathan bad when he was a little boy,' said Ma, 'like Nate said in court he did. I can't remember Pa hitting him, no more than is right and proper when a man is raising a boy. But Nate would never do what his Pa said, nor what I said, he always had his own way of doing everything. He treated us like we didn't know nothing. We was proud of his learning, but he would always use it against us. He acted like he thought because I couldn't read so good nor write that meant I was no better than a mule. Your Pa could read, and when he first started out he would help Nathan with his letters, but as soon as Nate could read better'n Pa he would use it against him any way he could. He was always using fancy words he knew we didn't know. And he was always talking about leaving the farm to go work on a newspaper or something. Pa and I knew after I had you I couldn't have no more, Sissy, and he was awful scared Nate would leave and there wouldn't be nobody to pass the farm on to. Nate said he would stay, but anytime he couldn't have his own way he would start threatening to leave.

'And then he found out what got Pa real mad. He found it in one of his books he was always reading, or the newspapers he would buy from the trading boat, that weren't full of nothing but evil as far as I could see. He said one day, why did he have to stay here if he had a mind to go some place else, said if he couldn't go work for anybody he wanted to work for he was no better off than a slave. He said maybe that was why Pa went to fight in Texas, because everyone knew that the war against Mexico was only fought to keep the niggers in their place, and that maybe he thought if slavery was all right for them it was all right for his own son, too.

'Well that got your Pa real mad. He never liked to talk about the War and the things he'd seen, and he knew what we'd all suffered, coming thousands of miles past Indians and wild beasts and through cold and hunger, scraping around in the dirt at the end of it, and all for what? So we could get a stake to get our own place up here, so your Pa would have a farm to pass on to his only son. To your Pa that was the greatest thing a man could do, to leave land to his son, he knew it was that and only that meant we never could be treated like slaves, that it was only the earth under your feet and the fact that you owned it and were beholden to no man for your bread, that's what made you free, wasn't no fancy words in the Constitution did that.'

'Why didn't Pa tell all this to Nate?'

'He tried to, he tried, he told Nate everything he'd learned in books about the Mexican War, or whatever some hothead abolitionist had written about it, that was all lies, that what mattered was whether a man owned land, and that's why they fought down in Texas, not to keep the black man slave but to make the white man free. He wouldn't say no more than that. He wasn't proud of that war or what he done in it. And he didn't like to see any man, black or white, in chains. Then how is a man supposed to feel, he works hisself half to death to leave a farm to his only son and that boy turns round to him and accuses him of treating him like a slave?

'So when Nate found out how to make Pa madder'n Hell, instead of trying to calm Pa down he did his best to keep him just as angry as he could do, and that was the first real bad beating I remember Nate had. After that it was like Nate wanted to be beaten. Pa tried to control hisself and I did my best to stand between 'em, but Nate would have his beatings come Hell or high water.

'It was like that the day he killed him. He stood there and he said he was treated worse than a slave and Pa hit him, Nate went to his room and come back with his things packed in a bag and they was cussing at each other and Nate saying he was leaving, going away for good, then your Pa went toward him, I don't know if he was going to hit him, I just don't know, Nate kind of had him over a barrel cause he knew if he was set on leaving there wasn't nothing he could do to stop him, then Nate picked up that fire iron and he hit his Pa just as hard as he could on the head and killed him.

'So you go to Nathan now and you tell him how hard Swann uses you and how I ain't no kind of mother and how I turned against my own son and you sit there with him and close your mind to that he murdered his own Pa, don't ask him neither how come a man never lifted his hand to you or to me should act that way toward his son, maybe you and him can find something in those books you is both reading says it's fine and good to kill your father or do most anything else comes into your head, but the only book I ever saw or took heed of says you should honour your father and your mother and it says you shouldn't kill, you hear me Sissy, you shouldn't kill at all.'

Ma stopped, her tears were talked away and she was burning with a flame that fired away the darkness, she wasn't in that darkness, she was burning and glowing with what she'd wanted to say so long, and I stepped toward her, toward that flame, scared of her but wanting her, too, till I heard her say, from out the flame,

'Don't you come near me, child, don't you come near me then go to him and have him tell his lies and you believe them, just go.'

I still didn't move. She turned her eyes on me, terrible and white like a winter storm, burning bright like a torch over ice, and said it again,

'Go.'

7

With Child

I was scared of another baby, and tried all I could think of to stop it from happening. There were ways Swann liked to use me I knew wouldn't get his seed where it needed to go, and though I hated them worse than when he took me in the natural way a man takes a woman, I tried to get him to use me those ways whenever I could. There was no use, though, in trying anything required his help. He was like a wild animal when the lust was on him and in any case, as he never said a word nor threw a glance at either of the children, didn't care how many I bore. I couldn't ask Ma about it outright, and didn't have no-one else to ask, but it didn't take her long to guess what was on my mind. All women must have had cause to think on these things, I suppose.

I tried everything she said. I put my grandy rags under my pillow and I ate some dust Ma made from a chicken's gizzard. I ate gunpowder and, on Saturday nights, rubbed it into my nipples, though Ma said this was only good after the baby was inside you and you wanted to stop it from growing and getting born. None of it did no good. By late summer I was with child again and so miserable and fearful of the future I could not keep from my face the sad expression that so enraged Swann, whenever he saw it, that he would cuss me and beat me.

Even after I found out a baby was coming I tried to get rid of it, drinking water that had had rusty nails stand in it. I even tried rubbing quinine and turpentine on myself, but I couldn't face the hot salt water and other, worse things that Ma said some women had used on the trail. Even if it worked, Ma told me, the women didn't always survive. She'd heard tell of too many horrors, of women dying in terrible pain, to help me that way. So I let it grow, knowing all the time that the miracle of life was being mocked, that no good could come from my swollen belly.

Fall was coming on and I was glad of the dark when I went to meet Nate. With the help of a little flour it covered the bruises on my face. Ma carried on doing her best to protect me but Swann was growing wilder and wilder. He worked harder than ever on the farm, stayed out longer than ever after his Saturday nights, and used me more than ever in his bed. He drunk more than a quart of whisky every day and killed more game than Ma and I could eat or salt away. I knew something bad would end it, but I thought the child inside me might protect me from his worst. Most of the time he was careful only to hit me in the face or on my arms where it wouldn't hurt my baby.

If the child inside me stayed his hand at all, though, it only made him find other ways to hurt and humiliate me. He would make me walk naked around the house if Ma wasn't around, make me serve him his meal with my growing belly sticking out before me, and if I tried to cover my shame he would take my wrist and twist it, or squeeze my arm until it bruised, all the time laughing at me until, if I carried on trying to resist, his humour would suddenly change and he would strike me, hard, across the face.

Once, late at night, he called for me to bring his whisky. When I brought it he poured out a full cup and told me to drink it. I'd never tasted it, but the smell of it in the jar and on his breath had always turned my stomach. I hesitated, made no move toward the cup.

'Drink it,' Swann said, and I knew from his tone that if I didn't do like he said he would beat me bad. I picked up the cup, all the time his eyes burning into me, and put it to my lips, but before I could take any of the foul stuff into my mouth I gagged and had to take the cup away, get the overpowering stench of it away from me.

Swann stood up, called me a name, grabbed me and held my neck under his arm like he was wrassling. He picked up the cup and forced it to my mouth, but all he managed to do was choke me, so that I couldn't drink at all. He dragged me down to the floor, pulling at my hair, and while he held me down, lying on my back, poured the full cup down my throat. He filled the cup twice more and forced it into me, all the time laughing like a devil.

I could hear the children stirring but knew that Annabel would be too scared to come out from behind the blanket that curtained off their bed from the room. Swann dragged me into the bedroom, then, still pulling at my hair, and forced me on to my stomach. I thought that I was going to die when the whisky took hold and the bed seemed to move like water under me. When he pinned me to it and used me, more cruelly even than was his habit, my stomach seemed to pull itself inside out and a brown mess, fouler even than had come from the jar, came out of my mouth, but Swann didn't pay it no mind.

All I could think of, through the pain and horror of it all, was that I wished to God, to Ma's God maybe, that the whisky would kill my baby and spare it from becoming another victim of the madness of its father, the weakness of its mother, or the terror of the world.

* * *

Winter come and I had to stop seeing Nate. Something about having the baby inside me made me take fright at the woods and the river at night, and I felt so weary to my bones that even the prospect of seeing Nate couldn't make me want to walk out in the darkness. I knew that I wouldn't be able to wait for him in the cold and darkness with as light a heart as I had done before. Some nameless fear was growing in me that took away my strength, the kind of strength you need to sit alone on a rock on the riverbank in the dead of a cold night, listening to the movements of night creatures and wondering if our Indians, who never caused us trouble, would start to, or whether a hungry bear might smell me out. The fears were only half real, sitting as I did on land my Ma had deeds to and less than a mile from the house, places I'd known in daylight since I was a little girl, and always with a shotgun to protect me, a shotgun I knew how to use as well as any man could, and almost as well as Ma, who'd taught me.

I told Nate I was with child and might not get down to meet him again until winter was over. He seemed relieved; I guessed the journey by horse and boat was wearing on him, too. He said he would write me, send the letter by the trading boat, which was all right because Swann never came down to the boat, preferring to buy his things in town. Him and Mr Packer didn't get along.

In fact, Swann seemed somehow scared of Mr Packer, like he sometimes did of Ma. I only ever saw them together once, and it was while Ma and me were down at the boat one day, not long after after Annabel was born. Mr Packer had some rolls of cloth out and was showing them to us, spreading them in his hands so that the sunlight caught the colours. Swann just strode on to the boat and said to me,

'Give the child to her,' meaning Ma, 'and come on up. I need you out to the field.'

I didn't want to go. It wasn't leaving Annabel, which I was used to, being as Swann would always put hisself before her, even if she needed to be fed or cleaned up. It wasn't that, now, because she was sleeping soundly and wouldn't have woke if I'd given her to a grizzly to hold. It was only that I didn't want to leave the boat, when the boatman came I could pretend for a little while that my life was normal, that I was like any housewife buying in things for her home and family. So, like with the whisky, I hesitated, even though I knew that it would always mean a beating, and that if Swann couldn't beat me right away, it would be worse for me when he had me to hisself again.

Ma saw me stand my ground and said to Swann,

'You go on back up, Sissy'll be along in a little while.'

I looked at her, grateful for her helping me. I could see Mr Packer, too, still holding the cloth, looking at Swann, watching him. He was smaller than Swann and leaner, and he looked like what he was, a storekeeper, but he looked too like he was taking Swann's measure, and that having taken it, he wasn't scared of him at all.

Swann glared at Ma and cussed.

'She'll come right now,' he said, and when I didn't move he cussed again.

Mr Packer laid the cloth carefully on the clean deck. He took a step toward Swann and said,

'Mister, if you want to use that kind of language in front of your own womenfolk there ain't much I can do but not like it, but my wife is just back there in the stores, and can hear every word, so I'll thank you to keep a civil tongue or go ashore.'

Swann looked at him, I was scared that he would take Mr Packer by the throat, that he might even kill him, but Swann only looked, his face expressionless, and he didn't say a word. He turned his gaze on me for a second, and I

77

knew what the look meant well enough, or what it would mean when he was in drink and had me to hisself. He cussed again, loud, like a boy learning how, then turned and left the boat. I expected a beating when I got back, but I went straight out to the field after we left the boat and worked with him till it was time to cook, and he never said a word to me.

Nate did write me, and I could write him back, too, and give it to the boatman to take. I had to remember not to use Nate's real second name, so that he couldn't be connected with us or with the killing he'd done. I'd never wrote a letter before, and when I wrote my first, which must have been about twenty words long, I felt as proud and weary as Mrs Stowe must have when she got through with Uncle Tom.

I could spell Sissy now, too, but I still didn't have no idea how you wrote Elizabeth. Sissy didn't seem right on a letter, somehow, though Nate would use it, so I used to sign them 'Your loving sister' and leave it at that. Even after Nate finally wrote my full name at the start of one of his letters I felt somehow shy of it, and instead of copying it down straight away I seemed to forget all about it, carrying on signing myself in the same way. It seems strange, now, but after all I still was hardly more than a child, for all the things I'd suffered.

Winter seemed long with the baby growing inside me. It is a mercy, though, to be with child in the cold time when the work ain't so hard nor the air so scarce. I waited, waited for the baby to come and for when I could see Nate again hard after it. I didn't dare ask Ma if Nate could come in the house. He wrote me a letter each month and I wrote one back. Neither of us said too much, though, we didn't really have the way of writing letters like I have seen and learnt how since, there was an awkwardness to them as if we hardly knew each other.

Nate talked about work, told me about books he'd read, and of a dance he went to one night.

'You wouldn't have recognised me hopping around the floor of that big barn, or striding and stepping with a lady on my arm and the fiddler playing "Turkey in the Straw" or the old "Zip Coon" song,' was what he wrote, but I could no more imagine it than I could see in my head a picture of New York City or the towns over the ocean where more people live than in the whole of California and the Territories put together. I only knew about such things because Nate told me, and they had less to do with real life, or what could be real, than the fairy stories my Ma had told me when I was a little child. Not that I ever thought what Nate said wasn't true, only that I could see the King of the Sea and the Prince of the Island, I could make a picture in my head of fairies and goblins and trolls, but hard as I tried I could not see a city or a railroad or a barndance.

I told Nate mostly about the children. There was so little in my life, and so much I had to avoid, for fear of making Nate sad, or mad enough to come after Swann, and for fear of feeling I'd betrayed Ma. Then I couldn't write so good as he could, anyway.

8

Winter Again

I lost my baby one Sabbath night near the end of the year. Swann didn't come back till it was near dark. He was still drunk and stunk worse than he ever had. Ma put some food in front of him and he ate it and called for another plate. His voice sounded strange, like when you are sick in the throat. When I tried to see what he was thinking all I could see in him was this evil that hated me and my baby and every living thing. I didn't want the children near him, sent them into Ma's room where they slept now, out of his way. They would've cried usually if I'd sent them off to bed so soon, but that night they went without a murmur. Ma went after them to take them some milk and see them off to sleep, but she didn't want to be around neither.

I got him his food and waited by him, case he wanted another plate. He called four times for more, till the pan stood empty and there was hardly a mouthful of cornbread for me and Ma. All the time he was drinking whisky.

When he'd eaten his fill he grabbed my arm and pulled me into the room where our bed was. He pulled off my clothes, tore my shift, and made me lay that way on the bed, naked with my belly sticking out, while he undressed. Then he stood in front of me and started to tell me all kinds of dirty things about what he had done to a whore in town, and how he was going to do the same to me. I had never heard him talk so much.

I started to cry and I couldn't hear him no more. I don't know why, I knew he was talking but I couldn't make out his words. I could hear him getting mad, hear his voice rising, and I tried to hold myself up thinking maybe this would help me understand him.

I saw him come at me, he was calling me bitch and other names worse than that, I felt the first blow hit me right hard in the middle of my belly, but after that I didn't hardly feel them. I could feel him hitting me on the belly and breasts, I could hear him cussing me, but I couldn't feel no pain no more, no pain at all.

Then it came back, a wave of the most awful agony, moving up through my body, seeming to tear me apart like a gutted fish. Just as suddenly, the hurt subsided again and I lay on the bed, could hear my sobs and smell my blood like the breath of Hell. The pain hit me again and I felt like I'd been thrown into the air, couldn't hear nothing but a distant cry like a bird in the night, or a small forest creature being taken by an owl. And again, the pain was gone. Then I could hear Ma's voice and see her pulling at his arms, hear Swann growl like an animal, and the pain come back to me once more.

I seen him hit Ma, not hard but just once across the face like he hit Nate that time, then he was gone and I thought Ma was gone too, but I could feel her arms and her hands on me somewhere through the pain, then I couldn't feel anything again and I was in the darkness, Swann's face was spinning in the darkness and I was falling into it, falling into his eyes that were blacker than the dark around them, his pale face the only thing I could see, falling, falling into his murderer's eyes that I knew had killed my baby and that I knew would kill me, soon as Annabel was old enough to whore for him when it weren't Saturday night and he come back from the field, with his belly empty and his mad eyes full.

I was lying in the tub we used to put before the stove and I could feel Ma's hands washing me and feel the good feeling of the warm water soothing me and I wondered why Ma wasn't mad at me for falling asleep in the tub and why I hurt so inside. I wanted to shake myself and wake and stand up so Ma wouldn't get mad, but I felt so warm and peaceful there in the water in the tub before the stove. I could hear Pa calling to Pirate outside, calling to him in his deep warm voice that sounded like the smell of the tobacco he smoked in his pipe. I felt so happy in the tub with Ma washing me with the warm, warm water, warm as Pa's voice and Pirate's fur, but I wondered still why I hurt inside, and how I could feel so happy when I hurt so bad, and why Ma didn't say, in her voice she used like she was mad but you knew she wasn't really mad at all, why she didn't say, Come on now Elizabeth Sleepytop, are you going to fall fast to sleep in that tub, because you know what will happen if you do, then I would say, pretending I was more asleep than I was, What will happen Mamma? and she would say, Why, the water will go cold and you will sink under it and the King of the Sea will swim up from his kingdom in the icy green depths and he will carry you away for his wife. Then I would say, But I don't care because Pirate will swim on down to rescue me, you just throw old Pirate in the tub and he will do that, if you ever saw Pirate in Tennant's Creek, Mamma, you know he can swim as good or better'n the King of the Sea anyhow. Then Mamma would lift me out in a big towel and dry me and tickle me awake and say, Sure I saw Pirate in the creek but if you ever see him in the bathtub or any place there is a cake of soap you will not need to go to Jerusalem or the land where the Elephant

82

lives, because you will have seen wonders enough for one little girl's life.

This night I must've fallen asleep in the tub, I was lying in my bed and I could still feel that Ma was there, it was dark and I couldn't hear Pa no more nor smell his pipe and I couldn't feel him there, I couldn't hear Pirate's barking or Nate in his bed over the other side of the room. And I knew Pirate would be sleeping out by the barn and Pa would be sat by the stove, maybe dozing the way he does, and Nate would be sitting with a lamp at the table reading his books or a newspaper or writing in his journal, but I couldn't feel none of them, only Ma, and I felt awful lonely and scared even though I knew they was all there I wanted to see them all to sit on Pa's knee and feel his whiskers to ask Nate to show me his map of America and all the big cities and the names of the states and territories to lie inside Pirate's fur so that I could feel them all and know they were there, and even though I was so sleepy and hurt so bad I had to take hold of Ma and pull myself up and cry out for Pa and Nate and Pirate and Mamma, Mamma, Mamma and then I heared her saying, Hush, my baby, hush, it is only a bad dream but your Mamma is here with you, here with you, hush my baby, hush, hush.

Swann disappeared and was gone two weeks. I was trying not to hope he would never come back, because I knew he would. I was over the pain, or the worst of it, and I'd got up early morning to help Ma. I remember saying to her, Ma, do you think Swann will be back? and she said, Sure he will, baby, I remember her words and how sad she looked at me.

That was only the night before, or so I remember it, and then the very next morning there he was standing in the doorway, not roaring, but sober and kind of quiet. Ma said to him,

'You have some nerve, mister, coming back here.'

He didn't answer her mean like he usually did but just stood awhile, quiet, then said,

'I got a right here.'

Ma said,

'You do? And I suppose you got a right to near kill a woman that is with child, your child, and to kill your own baby ain't even born.'

Swann looked at her, then at me. He said,

'That dumb bitch is enough to drive any man mad enough to kill.'

'Then just kill us both, now, finish us, we ain't inclined to wait around,' and Ma turned to the stove and began to move the new loaves from the warming place into the oven.

When she'd finished Swann still hadn't said nothing, or moved from the doorway. He looked tired, felt different. I could feel a kind of fear behind his meanness, and even the meanness seemed no more real than a cloud, or as if he was pulling it around him like a coat in the winter chill. It was like now I knew he could kill me and would if he had a mind, now I knew there wasn't nothing he wouldn't do, nothing too mean, I don't know why, I wasn't scared of him no more. And because he stood there and could feel I wasn't scared, he didn't know no more what to do. After a while he said, again,

'I got a right here.'

Ma didn't say a word. She lifted her work basket from out the corner and put it on the table. She took out a pair of James's pants and began to sew a patch on the knee where they'd come through. We were all silent. One of the children stirred in sleep. It was late and I knew that soon they'd wake.

Swann looked at me, hard, but it was as if the meanness and lust had drained away from him in weariness. The evil in him was looking to lay down to rest, but I knew when it had it would come back stronger than ever. I ain't never seen no god, but I prayed to something, prayed he'd go and leave us.

Swann walked past me, without looking again at me or Ma, into the room where he'd shared my bed. We heard some noises, like he was breaking something, not in one of his spells but slow, slowly breaking something open. Then we heard a shot and James woke behind the curtain where they slept and started to cry.

My heart jumped right up inside me, for a minute I thought he'd shot hisself dead but right away I knew better, knew better than that something as rotten as Swann would end itself that way.

Ma looked up from her sewing and said, quiet and kind of tired,

'What craziness is he doing now?'

I went over and picked James out of his bed. I whispered to Annabel, who was half woke up and looking scared,

'It ain't nothing, just your Pa set his gun off by accident.'

Then I turned around to see Swann come back into the room and stride across it toward the door and out into the winter sun. Ma and me looked at each other and I carried James over to the door in time to see Swann mounted and riding away over the hard snow.

James wriggled in my arms to be put on the floor. I let him down and walked back over to the sleeping room, the room where Swann had killed my baby and beaten and used me for so long.

The bed was pushed away from where it usually stood under the window and the boards prized up under it. The window was open and the cold air blew in. A strong-box stood on the sill, open and with its lock shot away. I thought how Swann always carried all his money around with him and how if he had some hid away like that it must have been a real lot, and when I thought about that and how he had took it and rode off like that I felt so full of joyousness and smiles that I started as if I'd turn around in a little dance like I'd do when I was a child, but somehow I couldn't start the dance, my feet just lost their strength and my legs went like the legs of a new-born calf and I stepped over to the bed, sat down on it hard and when the tears started to come I felt Ma's arms around me and felt Annabel pulling at my dress and heard her say,

'What is it Mamma, why you crying Mamma?' and Ma saying to Annabel, that it was all right,

'Mamma's been awful sick, baby, but now she's well, now she's well, and sometimes when you get well like that you just have to cry.' Then she said,

'Go see what James is in to in my kitchen, Annabel,' and she pulled me to her and held me while I cried against her breast like a hungry child.

I waited a week, and just like before when I knew he was coming back, but the hope that he wasn't wouldn't leave me, so this time I couldn't shake off the feeling that one day I would look up from a piece of sewing and there he would be, standing in the doorway blocking out the sun. Still in my heart I knew this time that Swann had gone away, far away, and that if he ever came back it would not be for a long time, and that by that time things might have changed, we might be stronger, more able to defend ourselves and our own from his evil.

We would be all right for the winter, stores a-plenty to last us through, even though Swann had left us without a penny. Ma and me didn't speak much during that week, we both knew there were questions we'd have to answer, that if

Swann was gone we needed to talk again about things would be full of pain for both of us.

It was late at night, the house was warm and quiet with the kind of peace you get when a cold wind is blowing outside and there are logs enough for the fire. Ma was sitting by the stove, silent and still in the darkness, nothing lit but a single lamp to save oil and see us to the spring. I stood for a while in the doorway of the room where I slept now with James and Annabel, all in the one bed for the warmth of it. I'd changed into my nightdress and let down my hair to brush it, and I took up the brush now and ran it through the long dark strands that fell down over my breast. I caught myself wondering if I was pretty, a thing I hadn't thought about for years and years, since before Swann came. Ma had her back to me, but I could feel a kind of peace in her, too, and I felt a sudden sadness that Nate weren't there to share the warmth and quiet. So I walked over and put my hands on Ma's shoulders and kissed her hair. I walked around her and sat on the other side of the stove, and I knew Ma was thinking that I was sitting in the place Pa would've been in if he'd still been with us. I felt kind of shy of speaking, thinking on that, but I gathered myself up and looked over at her and said,

'Ma, I want to write a letter to Nate.'

She looked at me, smiled a strange kind of smile I couldn't read nor see behind, and said,

'I guess I am cursed to have nothing but book-learning children. You think I don't know you been writing to him?' She looked at me, and when I looked back at her I could see she understood.

'I guess this letter will be different to those, child, is that what you're telling me?'

She didn't say it unkind, but with a feeling like she would have to give way, now, that if I wanted to write this letter to Nate then that is what would happen, that if I was going

87

to ask him to come back she would have to let me do it. I knew she thought she was old and the world was not hers to tell no more.

She smiled again and shook her head, but there was love in her smile and no scolding nor hardness in her face. Even in the dim lamplight I could see its soft outlines. I wanted to tell her how good she looked, how proud Pa must have been to have her for his bride. She said,

'And what will you say in this here letter?'

I'd been thinking about this ever since Swann rode away, so I said,

'Well, Mamma, I guess what I'd like is to ask him to quit working for Mr Turner and come home.'

Ma was quiet. She lifted her hand to her cheek and stroked it, gazing all the time into what had gone before. I looked away from her but tried to watch her all the same, leaning my head into the brush as I pulled it through my hair. After a long time she said,

'I don't know, Sissy.'

'What don't you know, Ma?' I asked her.

More quiet, and the wind getting higher outside. Looking out the window I could see snow begin to fall. Somewhere in the distance I thought I heard the sound of hooves, but then I listened again and knew it was only the rattling of the door on the barn, the clanking noise the pump made in a high wind, the nervous shuffling of the animals in the night. I shivered a little and leaned nearer the stove.

Ma said,

'Well, in the first place, I don't know whether I want Nathan here. Then, we don't know for sure that Swann won't come back, and now Nathan has been out of jail so long and working and all, maybe he won't let hisself be run off so easy this time. In which case Swann will kill him.'

'Maybe he will kill Swann, Ma,' I said, though I felt

foolish when I said it, like you would think of a child who says her Pa can fight anybody and beat them.

But Ma didn't laugh the way she might have done, the way I suppose I thought she would, she didn't look at me that way she does when she thinks I am dreaming fools' dreams, she only shrugged and said,

'Maybe. Who knows what they might do? But if Nate kills Swann they will likely hang him, being as he has killed a man before.'

She looked at me, expecting me to speak, but I didn't want to say nothing, didn't want her to set to thinking about Pa, turn herself against Nate coming home.

'Anyway, Sissy,' she said, and she shook her head and looked away from me, down toward the floor, then back at my face, straight at my face,

'I don't want no more killing here, even if it was Swann that was killed.'

'So how we going to get along, Ma? With no man and four mouths to feed, how we going to get along?'

'Now, Sissy, hold on,' Ma said, 'I didn't say I wouldn't have Nate back. I'm just thinking about it, is all. Give me a little time, child, give me a little time.'

I didn't feel good doing it, like I didn't feel good the time I made Nate tell me about Pa, but I had to know what Ma wanted, what she would allow, I had to know if we were all going to be back here, working together and eating together and laughing and raising our young. I knew Ma wanted that too, if only her pride and hurt would let her.

'How much time, Ma?' I asked her.

She sighed, a long, weary sigh came from way down inside her, and wrung her hands together in her lap. Then she stood up and walked over to the table where the lamp stood. Her back to me, she said,

'I'm going to my bed, Sissy, should I turn out the lamp?'

'No, Ma, leave it just a little while, so's I can take a look at Annabel and James,' I answered her.

She turned, the lamplight playing shadows on her face. I could feel that love and hate fighting for her, fighting behind the shadows that threw light and dark across her eyes and the silver tips of her hair.

'Write your letter to Nathan, Sissy,' she said, and when she saw the happiness jump to my face she held up her hand and said, 'but hold on. Don't tell him we want him back here. Tell him that Swann is gone, maybe for good but we ain't sure, tell him we'd be happy to have him ride on over here one Sabbath and break bread with us, now Swann ain't here to stop him, but don't say nothing about wanting him back. Give me time to think it over, and give us a chance to see how Nathan acts when he thinks we need him. I have been beholden long enough.'

'Nate ain't like Swann, Ma,' I told her.

'No, child, he ain't,' Ma replied, 'but just what he is like I don't know yet. I been blaming him for a bad thing he done ten years ago, and for the lies he's still telling and maybe believing about it. But here he might do good or bad, as any man might that had two women who need his hands and his back, so we'll see whether there's good in my son or whether maybe he only ain't so mean as Swann because he ain't so big.'

I remember the letter I wrote Nate, pretty well, though the spellings weren't as good as I can manage now. It was a short letter, shorter than most of the others, but even harder to write. It read something like this,

My dear brother Nathan,
    Swann is gone away from the farm for a long time,
    maybe for good, so Ma says as you and him don't get along

this would maybe be a good time to pay us a visit
one Sabbath. We will be waiting for you every Sabbath now
and will set an extra place at table,

    Your loving sister,
    Elizabeth

I read the letter out to Ma and she said it was okay. She laughed when I read that about Swann and Nate not getting along, but I put that in so Nate could think that. He could say to hisself he got a Ma and sister near enough but he don't visit them because he don't get along with his brother-in-law. He could even say that to other people if they asked. It can't be easy for a man to admit he don't visit his folks cause his sister's man drove him off their place and his Ma don't want to see him anyhow.

I read the letter over and over, to make sure I had it just right, and only then did I realise that I'd done what I'd set out to do when I wrote my first ever word, I'd written my name full and right, Elizabeth, and when I looked at it I felt somehow for the first time that I knew exactly who I was and what I was for.

9

Spring, 1868

That was a week I will remember, with the cold easing and the thaw turning the ice to mud and the children feeling how happy I was and taking it in and seeming to be laughing all day and sleeping sound all night. Annabel found the boatman's toy she had forgotten, the way children will, so that it was like getting it again anew, and she would make it spin for James and see his eyes grow big as hers watching the colours turn to white. I was praying the thaw would stay gentle so the mud wouldn't block the roads nor the river flood, or that it would not plunge again into cold to stop Nate spending his Sabbath here.

And then it came, the morning bright and clear, cold again but not so cold to stop a man riding twenty miles, and no snow nor sleet nor storm in the air or the sky. I knew Nate would come, knew he would ride in early to tell us when he was going to come to start his new life with us, all together again, ready for the planting time when we could all work and lay the good seed in the earth.

And I thought how we would harvest our corn and beans and of the vegetables we would grow and how we would sit out winter, three chairs by the stove, and Ma with forgiveness for Nate sitting with him by the fire, sitting all together, blood and blood, and how maybe someone would start a school and Nate would ride over to meet Annabel and she would run out, pretty as a picture in her school dress, a book in her little hand, and she would shout to him, Uncle Nathan, Uncle Nathan, she would shout, and he would pick her up in his arms and twirl her round and set her on the buggy and ride home.

I could see it all in pictures like the pictures in a book and I could smell it too and even taste it, dry in the back of my throat, taste it like you can taste good food when you sit at table and it ain't ready and you have to wait, hungry when you are a child, but with a hunger that you know is going to end in a full belly and a warm bed.

And then he was there, we heard the hooves of his horse first on the hard ground, he could ride here all the way now and not row softly upriver like a pirate from a story, the sound of his horse the sound of freedom and power. When we heard it we ran out the house, Annabel and me at the door looking up the road toward where we knew he would be coming, seeing him dark against the sun, and Ma still sitting at table, peeling some potatoes for our meal, knowing it was him and thinking how she would be killing that chicken for Nate at last, but too proud and stubborn to stand up, waiting for him to walk into her house and wash away the stain of what had come between them.

It was the finest feeling to sit at table with Ma and Nate, the children watching him and watching me and knowing something was going to happen but not knowing what. Ma had cooked up the best meal she knew how with what we had, she had bought things from the trading boat, bought them on promises to make up clothes: dried fruits and maple sugar, hot spices and the best coffee beans, even some chocolate and a jug of hard cider, things we hadn't seen on the farm, or hardly, since Pa's time.

Nate was laughing a lot and telling us stories about being a cowboy on Mr Turner's farm, about how Mr Turner had had the governor stay over one night and all the ladies from around had come in fine dresses with their husbands. Nate was being what he was best at, telling these funny stories, describing the ladies so's you could see their faces and how they moved, how the governor had a face just like a bull dog and his wife looked like a catfish, he could make his face look like those things and make us all laugh doing it, even Ma. I hadn't heard Annabel laugh so much before and James who didn't really understand could feel the happiness of it and laughed along too, pulled faces back when Nate did it to him, and even sat on Nate's knee when we had done eating and let him feed him off a spoon.

There was one story in particular, I wouldn't have even guessed that Annabel would've understood it, one of Nate's tall tales, and it made her laugh and laugh and for months after ask me to tell her again about the time Uncle Nate saw a talking bear. I never could tell it like Nate, but it always made Annabel laugh just the same.

The way it happened, Annabel told Nate that she wasn't allowed to go into the forest on her own, 'until I'm old enough to use a shotgun as good as Ma, on account of the grizzlies.'

'Very wise advice, young lady,' Nate said, and like always I could tell right away from his voice that there was a tall story coming.

'Them grizzlies is mean as devils. Till you civilise 'em, that is.'

'Civilise 'em, Uncle Nate?' Annabel said, getting her tongue in a knot on the unfamiliar word.

'Sure,' Nate told her. 'Grizzlies can be civilised just like Indians. Except it ain't quite the same. You know the difference between a regular Indian and a civilised Indian, Annabel?'

She shook her head, her eyes looking bigger than ever. Ma was grinning at Nate with an expression I'd hardly ever seen on her face, almost like when she was playing with the boatman's toy. She was having fun.

'Well, a regular Indian is mean to white folks. He's only friendly to other Indians. You civilise him, and he starts behaving more like white folks, that is, he's still as mean as ever to them, but he's mean to other Indians as well.'

Ma shook her head and carried on grinning. Annabel was waiting for the grizzlies.

'Tain't that way with bears though, Annabel,' he told her, using the serious voice I had heard so often in his stories. 'You civilise a grizzly, and he'll be gentle as a cow. He'll be so gentle, some folks just can't resist taking advantage of him.' Nate winked at me.

'For instance, I was in a saloon the other day,' he said, 'when in comes a grizzly size of the state house.'

'Weren't you scared?' Annabel asked him.

'No, ma'am,' Nate said. 'I wasn't scared none, because that grizzly was wearing overalls and a coon-skin cap, so's I could see right away he was as civilised as Old Abe Lincoln. Anyway, Mr Grizzly goes up to the bar-tender and he says, Gimme a beer. And the barkeep, you could see he was a mean one, fellow looked like a regular Democrat, he weighs the situation up and he knows these here civilised bears are gentle as kittens and none too bright, so he gives him a beer and says, That'll be a dollar.'

'A dollar!' Annabel says. 'Ain't that a hundred pennies?' And we all laughed.

'It sure is, Annabel, a hundred pennies, far too much to spend on one glass of beer. But the grizzly is new in town and he don't want no trouble, so he pays his dollar. Then the bar tender starts to feel a little guilty, as people usually will when they've done wrong, and he wants to be friendly to the grizzly. So he says to him, Sure is a strange thing, sir, but we don't get too many of your kind in here. And the bear looks back at him and says, Friend, I ain't complaining but at a dollar a glass of beer I ain't hardly surprised.'

And Nate burst right out laughing, Ma too, while Annabel said,

'Did it happen, did it really happen, Grandma?' but Ma was laughing too much to say, not laughing at the story now but at Annabel's half-believing it.

James watched everyone laughing and it made him laugh, too, and when I looked at them all it made my heart feel hot with love for them and my blood race with hope that this would be the first of a thousand Sabbaths watching the children grow in warmth and happiness, and that the sound of laughter, hardly heard before, would come to fill our home and fill our days.

All the time, though, I was trying to see into Nate and I couldn't, I could just see enough that I knew something wasn't how I'd thought it was going to be. I tried to put the feeling away, to see Nate's smile and not look at the face behind it, not look inside the face to see where Nate was hid, to listen to his laughter and let it drown out the other noise, the noise I could hear of some great sorrow, the sorrow you hear in the howl of a wolf or the cry of its prey, I couldn't tell which.

When Ma and me had cleared the table and still nothing had been said about why Nate was there, he looked around the room and breathed in deep, like he was trying to know the house again, trying to see through what had been, to a time before the awful things that had happened here had come to pass, and he said,

'Ma, that was I think about the best meal I ever ate. And

now I think I'd like to take a stroll around outdoors, being as it's coming a little warmer, and maybe see it all down with a cigar.' And then he looked at me and said,

'You gonna join me, Sissy?'

I didn't know rightly what I should say, what Ma would want, but I knew Nate wanted to talk over things with me, maybe find out more about how the land lay before he spoke to Ma, so I said,

'Well, Nate, I can't just leave Ma to do all the dishes when she done most of the cooking.'

But Ma said, 'Oh, Sissy, you go show Nathan around like I know you want to, and Annabel here will help me clear up.'

Annabel started to object, because I suppose she thought taking a walk with Uncle Nate would be more fun than washing dishes with her Grandma, but Ma gave her one of those looks could even put a stop to Swann, and she shut up.

Soon as we got out past the barn Nate asked me how I'd lost my baby.

I said,

'Oh, you know, I was lifting something heavy and I fell down, and . . . ' but it didn't sound true even to me, and Nate put his hand on my arm, and he said,

'He beat you, didn't he Sissy, he beat you so bad you lost your baby, ain't that it?'

I swallowed to clear the dryness in my throat and nodded. Nate cussed and looked away, across the field toward the forest and hills and the river where we used to meet.

I said, 'Don't pay it no more mind, Nate, Swann's gone now and I just know he ain't coming back. Baby's better off not being than having that for a pa. And now Swann done that, now he's gone, Ma will let you come back to us, I know she will, if you talk to her she might not say you can come back, she might not say it straight away, that's just her pride doing that, but I can feel it in her she's already made up her mind to let you.' I spoke fast, unable to stop the excitement and hope in me from showing itself.

Nate stood away from me a little and stopped, facing me. If I looked past him I could see the mountains in the distance and the high ground above Tennant's Creek, where we had both played as children, jutting out of the forest. It was sunny and clear, the edge of chill had gone from the air and greenness was beginning, starting to take over from the blacks and whites and browns and duller greens of winter and the mudtime that followed. Nate said,

'I don't think I can come back here, Sissy.'

I felt like I did when Swann had hit me in the belly, a sharp pain then numbness and nothing, emptiness and nothing at all. I looked at Nate, quickly, then I looked at the ground that fed us, and I couldn't see nothing in either place, no green hiding in the ground, and nothing in Nate but a wall he'd put there to stop me seeing, a wall of mud like the cold hard ground that spring hadn't come to yet, that was waiting for the sun to do its work.

'Is it because of Ma?' I asked him, but he could hear the hope in my voice and shook his head at that, not hard but in a way that said he'd made up his mind.

We began to walk again, slowly now and in no particular direction, just for the moving of it, the keeping warm and the moving.

'I ain't saying I wasn't hurt when Ma didn't want me here, but that ain't it. If that's all there was to it, then I guess I'd let it go and try to meet her halfway. It wouldn't be so warm and easy as you think or hope, Sissy, there's a lot of bad between me and Ma, bad that won't melt away with the last of the snow just because you're too young to remember everything that went on, and still less just because you want it to.'

I could see it inside him when he said that, past the wall he'd tried to build and right inside him, just exactly like before, that burning feeling of righteousness, that feeling of truth and pain that I'd felt in him when he told me about Pa and that I felt in Ma, too. And I wondered again how two people could tell me things that couldn't both have been, and yet both of them do it from inside this great spirit of truthfulness and righteousness, both of them making me feel the feeling I know I get when anyone is telling me true.

'Is it because you're scared of Swann?' I said that, even though I expected it to make Nate mad, but he stayed quiet and spoke slow, not rising up at all like I thought he might.

'That comes into it, sure,' he said, 'but that ain't all of it neither.'

'We need you here, Nate,' I told him. 'We need you to help us to protect ourselves if Swann comes back, and to feed ourselves if he don't.'

'Sure,' Nate said, 'so now Ma suddenly finds out I ain't so bad after all, I'm all of a sudden welcome back here, the long lost son.'

'You know that ain't how it is, Nate,' I said, and I said it quiet and sad, I felt like I ought to be mad with Nate for saying a thing so cruel, but when I looked into him there wasn't no cruelty in him, no more than there is in a crying child keeping you awake when you need your sleep bad.

Nate said nothing more for a while. We walked on across the field, into the sun, away now from the forest and the mountain, so that we could see out over the farmland and down the river toward Sacramento.

'Well I can't come back, anyhow, Sissy,' Nate said. 'I am afraid of Swann, but it ain't for me that I'm afraid.'

He reddened and looked down and seemed to stammer with the difficulty of finding his words.

'The fact is I have a sweetheart,' he said then, 'I've asked her if she'll be my wife and she says she will.'

I knew even when Nate told me that there was going to be suffering come out of it, suffering for me and my babies and for Ma, too, and I knew that what I'd wanted so long couldn't happen now, that I had been foolish to want it, to build up hope on it, to use it to sustain me through Swann and through the beatings he gave me, the pain he gave me, using the day when Nate would come home and Swann would be gone like other folks use heaven, or like that fairy story prince, to keep them from laying down there and right away dying just from having no reason to live. I knew all that then, but I didn't let myself feel that, didn't have to think about it, to look inside myself, but felt it instead pushed down under me, and jumped up to Nate, put my arms around his neck and cried out in joy for him. I wasn't faking it either, because I was young but I'd lived long enough to know that joy and happiness are as real as pain and sorrow, realer maybe, I wasn't faking but just pushing back inside myself the feeling of fear and panic I felt jump into my heart and kind of seep into the pit of my belly.

I kissed Nate and told him how happy I was for him and how I couldn't wait to meet her and asked him what she was called and how had he met her and a hundred other questions all at once, not waiting for answers but just letting this glad feeling, that seemed to come out of my fear without killing it, just letting it flow from me like water from a spring.

'She's called Marianne,' Nate told me, 'she works for Mr Turner, or rather for his wife. She's twenty-two years old. She has blonde hair and blue eyes.'

We walked back toward the house, Nate answering my questions, now, quiet and proud and more like, I don't know, more like a growed up man than he usually seemed to me.

'Is she pretty?' I asked him, teasing, and he teased me back, saying she had only one eye and, 'her teeth is brown from chawing tobacco and her fingernails all cracked and dirty on account of before she come here she was a miner in Eureka.'

Then I chased him back toward the house saying I would whup him, cause if he was going to marry he would have to get used to a woman whupping him, till he turned round, quick and sudden and caught me in his arms and held me for a moment, then stepped back from me and held both my hands, his arms stretched out like he wanted to take a good long look at me, and he said,

'Sissy, if there was a painter greater than all the painters ever lived he could paint you and he could paint Marianne and he would've painted all the beauty of the world, and Marianne would be day and you would be night.'

And I would've laughed at him to hear him talk so, the way you are supposed to laugh when someone starts to talk that way, to tell you you are pretty or beautiful or to talk poetry to you when you are just a farm girl not born to have such things said to you or about you, but I could see in Nate's face that he wasn't looking for me to laugh, he was talking from right inside him, talking his truth, that had been locked inside him in long lonely nights on the hard prison bunk, and in the fear and misery after Swann threw him out of his home and Ma seemed glad of it, and I looked at Nate when he said that and I put my hand to my long black hair, tied now behind my head, and I thought how it looked when it hung down over my breast, over the pale of my skin or the white of my nightdress, I looked into Nate's face and I smiled and bit my lip and thought about those things and heard inside my head my name, Elizabeth, and what Nate

101

had said, that I was dark and beautiful, like the night. I shook my head, as if he'd bought me a gift he couldn't afford, or one so precious I was scared to have it in my keeping.

Then I looked at Nate again and it had passed, the pictures of the night, the beautiful moonlit nights and times of gathering dark we spent out at Tennant's Rock on the river, had passed, and I was back in my time, wanting to know what Nate was going to do, wanting to make my own plans and needing to know what his were.

We turned and walked on toward the house. I said, carefully,

'Why can't you and Marianne come and live here, Nate?'

He didn't answer straight away, I could feel him tense and uneasy, picking his words.

'There ain't room, Sissy,' he answered.

'We could build.'

'That's true. But I don't know, or rather I do because I made up my mind before I rode over here. First, there's always the possibility Swann would come back and I can't put Marianne in that kind of danger.'

'We're in it, Nate,' I said, but I felt mean when I said that, and wished I hadn't.

We walked along for a while, neither of us speaking. We were nearly back at the barn when he stopped, the way you do when you want to finish something before you get to a place where there will be other people around. He said,

'I got my own life, Sissy. I lost ten years of it because of, well, it doesn't matter now what it was because of. When I come back I expected just to pick up, to take over the farm and work with Ma and you and your man, find myself a wife, maybe build another house for us. Land here could have fed us all, Sissy. But it didn't work out that way, and I can't one year be told to get off my own farm and the next to get on it again. If I bring Marianne back here Ma will never let us be. There will be three women and you will all have your own ways and I don't know, I don't think it would work out.'

What Nate said sounded well enough, but I could feel this unease in him again which wasn't there in the words. I wondered if he was ashamed of us.

'Will we meet her soon?' I asked him, wanting to know if there would be some way out of that for him, wondering if he'd try to keep Marianne away from his past. But he smiled and said,

'Sure. Now let's go on back to the house and tell Ma, then I'll tell you all about what we are going to do.'

As we walked back across the yard, Annabel ran out and grabbed Nate by the hand, James toddled out after her, laughing at something his Grandma had done I guess, but when he saw Nate he didn't stop, he went right on laughing and ran toward us. Then Ma came out, drying her hands on her apron, and taking it off so that she could sit with us in her Sabbath dress.

I don't think Ma allowed herself to feel the mixed up things I felt when Nate told her about his sweetheart. She knew straight away that he wouldn't be coming home, but she never had made up her mind that that would be a good thing anyway, and now she was maybe glad to have the deciding of it took from her.

Nate had already made all his plans to move him and Marianne up to Oregon, and they were intending to go there in less than a month. The wedding would be in three weeks, in Mr Turner's house. I hadn't been near people in so long that the idea of a wedding with lots of guests and maybe music and dancing scared me, though it excited me too.

'So when are you going to bring her to see us, son?'

Ma asked. I watched him, felt like my eyes were shining, wondered what he would say.

All he said was,

'A week from now, I guess, Ma,' and I felt surprised, somehow, that he wasn't talking poetry like he had before, that such ordinary words could describe something as exciting as this.

'Next Sabbath will be the best time for us, Ma, I think.'

'Next Sabbath, then,' Ma said, sounding satisfied, and it was settled.

When Nate rode away, Ma came to the door with us to watch him and when he turned to wave she waved back with the rest of us, and when I went in to keep James from some mischief he'd found and Annabel forgot her uncle and went off to look for the next thing her day would bring, Ma stood on the porch and watched, until Nate's horse and its rider disappeared round a bend in the road where it starts to rise toward the forest.

For the next two or three days after Nate's visit, Ma felt tight as a bowstring. Most of the time she was real happy, singing at her chores, playing all the time with the children, worrying about every little thing to do with Marianne, whether we could feed her as well as she would be used to at the Turner place, whether she would look at our dresses and wonder what kind of family she was marrying into, what she should call her.

'Nate never even told us her full name,' Ma said, 'and it would be just like a man not to do it even when he introduces us.'

'I'm sure she won't mind us calling her Marianne, Ma,' I said.

But Ma thought that wouldn't do, 'until we're acquainted. Your Grandma Holt never did call me by my given name,' she laughed at the memory of it. 'Even on the morning of my wedding day I was Miss Williams, then it was always Daughter. I guess times have changed a little at that, but I won't feel right calling her Marianne to her face.'

During the day she was all movement and noise, working twice as hard as usual and talking more than I'd ever heard her do before. When she wasn't worrying about the impression we would make on Nate's intended, she seemed as happy and as nervous as if it were her own wedding day she was waiting on. Only at night, when the children were abed and the lamp was lit, did she become more quiet, retreating into herself, thinking, I could see, of Pa, and maybe of her own wedding day.

We sat up late, neither of us able to sleep for the excitement of it, even though we were more wore out than ever. Anytime Annabel or James stirred in their sleep Ma would be up with the lamp to look at them, leaving me sitting in darkness by the stove. Then she would come back, smiling in an odd kind of way, as if at her own foolishness, and sit back down opposite me.

She wouldn't speak more than a word, maybe to say, 'It wasn't nothing, they're both sound asleep,' or, 'James has kicked away the quilt again, and his little feet are froze through,' then she'd sink back into her dreams. Aside from that, only if I asked her a question would she speak, and then just long enough to answer it in a distracted voice, as if her mind were still elsewhere.

'What are you thinking on, Ma?' I asked her more than once, or, 'You ain't still worrying about what Marianne likes to eat?'

And she would smile, and say, 'Nothing child,' or, 'I was just thinking how much Annabel has the look of my sister, Kate, who would have been your Aunt Katherine if the Lord hadn't taken her back to him.'

105

She felt full of love for us all but her mood seemed somehow gloomy, too, standing out against the girlish excitement she showed during daylight. Only once did she speak more than a few words, and that was when I asked her if she would come to the wedding.

She thought about it.

'I guess I will,' she said at last, 'though I don't know that I wouldn't be feared of a crowd of people after so long seeing no-one. And I never thought to see Nate married, after what he done. He still ain't repented of it, neither, but I think I can feel something in his heart, now, that will maybe grow into wisdom when he gets older. He's still pretty young, I guess, though he's no child.'

'Maybe Marianne will teach him to be good,' I said, trying to bring the talk away from Nate's crimes.

'You can't do it, Sissy, and if a man ever comes a-courting you, as I surely hope and pray he will, you'd better know that.'

I found myself blushing at her words, as if I'd never mothered two children and carried a third.

'He's either good or he ain't, though no man's all good and, fore Swann come, I'd've said none's all bad. If he's good then a woman who ain't a fool'll bring it out of him, and I pray Marianne's the woman to bring out whatever good there may be in Nate.'

'I just wish they weren't going so far away,' I told her. 'I know Nate's a good man, Ma, and I want to be there, near him and near you, when he shows it.'

Ma shook her head.

'Nate maybe is good, or has good in him,' she said, 'but he done as terrible a thing as a man can do, and he done it here. Maybe he was right to come back, to face us again, maybe he had to do that, though he don't seem able to face hisself with the real truth of it.'

I started to speak, but Ma hadn't finished.

'That don't matter, now. Whether he should've come back I don't know, but I know he's right to go away again. Nate's bright. Him and Marianne, if she is a good woman and not afraid to work, they can make something up there in Oregon never would happen here.'

I thought about what she'd said.

'I guess you're right, Ma,' I told her, though I wasn't really convinced of it, 'but it's going to be hard for us without him.'

Ma smiled, I don't know what at. She said,

'I won't say Nate don't owe us nothing, but I don't think he can pay it back in field-work. Maybe he can do it by living an honest life, and giving me some more grandchildren to add to those two in there.'

I smiled back, and Ma stood up slow, as if she were feeling her years. She walked over, put her hand on my shoulder, and spoke in a voice that was low but firm,

'I guess if you can pay back life at all, then that is the only way how. It's a tall order, Sissy, I guess you know that as well as I do.' She left me then, walked toward her room.

'Don't forget to douse the lamp,' she called to me, then stopped at her door. She spoke again without turning round. Her head was bowed, and she murmured low, as if only part of her wanted me to hear.

'We got along without your Pa, Sissy, and we been getting along since Swann left. I guess it will be hard, but when ain't it ever been?'

I watched her leave, took the lamp, and climbed into my bed alongside Annabel and James.

10

Letters and Lies

Dear Sissy (Nate wrote),

I sure did have a pleasant day with you and Ma.
I have told Marianne about next Sabbath and she is
real excited about meeting all of you. I am writing to
make sure Ma does not say anything to Marianne about
me and Pa. I think it is best to put the past behind me
and for Marianne not to know anything of those awful
things that happened so long ago. So please have a word
with Ma to that effect.

After next week I think I can maybe take some time off
here and come over and help you with the planting.

Your loving brother,
Nathan

Ma heard the letter out, then sat for a while without
speaking. I could feel when I was reading it that what Nate
was saying was upsetting her, but I had to concentrate so
hard on the reading I could not give it that much thought,
if I looked up at Ma I lost my place and stumbled over the
words. I felt guilty about this, as if I had put pride in my
reading in front of Ma's feelings, maybe in the way Nate
once had done. But the letter had to be read.

All Ma said when I'd finished reading was,

'So he wants me to lie for him again. This time I got to pretend not that he killed his Pa with good cause, but that it never happened at all. And it ain't to no judge I have to pretend this, to tell this lie, but to a young woman I don't even know who is going to marry my son, to put her life in his hands, to put her children's lives in his hands, a man who has killed and won't even admit to hisself what he has done.'

'Nate just wants to put the past behind him, Ma,' I said to her, echoing his own words from the letter, but it didn't sound true or right, not even to me.

'You don't put the past behind you by turning your mind from it, Sissy,' she said, and she spoke quietly and with her thoughts turned inwards, 'you only do it by repentance. Nate ain't repented nothing.'

I wanted to argue with her, to tell her she was wrong, just to make her feel better about Nate, to give her back the happiness and pride she had started to feel at last in him. But I knew I couldn't, knew there was no truth in it, I knew that Ma was right and that she had lied for him once and should not be asked to do it again.

When I'd first read the letter, I hadn't thought nothing of it. I only looked to Nate's happiness, and then to Ma's, and I suppose my own. But Ma listened to the letter, she looked inside herself and saw what she had been, she looked at me and how I'd had to live, and she thought first of all of Marianne, a woman she hadn't even met.

So when I looked at her, listened to what she said and listened to Nate's voice speaking through the words he'd written on paper and sent to me, I knew that Ma was being true and that Nate had failed us, failed to repent inside his heart, that he was now looking to leave us behind, that our pain was more than he could bear, that he would head up to Oregon with his bride he'd won in untruth and we would never see nor hear of him again. If he was to live with Marianne without her knowing of his past, then we, who lived inside it still, would needs be left to face as best we could whatever our truth would bring.

Ma's quiet, knowing anger was melting away into something like rage. She raised her voice, clenched her fist, you could see her face setting hard against her son, all the force of her rejection of him returning,

'And he puts that in about the planting,' she said, 'puts it in there like a threat, because he thinks in his pride we can't manage it without him. And you told me he wasn't nothing like Swann.'

Nate hadn't been able to give his letter to the boatman, because the boat wasn't due up this stretch of the river until the following week. He'd sent a boy over with it, a boy not much younger than myself, though still with the look of a child.

He had waited while we read the letter, lolling in the spring sunshine over by the pump, drinking a glass of root beer I'd given him.

'Any reply?' he asked when I came out.

I wondered whether he had heard raised voices, but there wasn't nothing in his tone that made me think he might be intruding on our pain. I could see him looking at me, almost like Swann used to but without the same meanness, a comical kind of look, really, but one which showed a desire in him, a desire which filled the empty spaces I could feel inside his tense and boyish soul. I guessed he didn't have a Ma, nor no-one else, and I wondered if he was the same boy Nate had met when he first went by Turner's farm.

'You hungry?' I asked him.

For some reason he laughed.

'Yes, ma'am,' he said, first time I'd ever been called that.

I told him I wanted to write a reply for him to take, and brought him a piece of pie to eat while he was waiting. He ate like I remembered Pirate doing, almost without chewing at all.

All I wrote to Nate was,

Dear Nathan, I need to see you before Sabbath.
Meet me at Tennant's Rock any night at dusk.
This is very important – don't fail me,
    Your loving sister,
    Elizabeth

I wanted to scratch out 'don't fail me', which I thought sounded too hard on Nate and too grand, and I tried my best to think of a word I could spell, to use instead of 'important', which must have been a sight to behold, but instead of standing puzzling over it all day I sealed it fast before I could change my mind about the whole thing.

I gave the boy the letter and watched him ride away. There seemed a sadness in the air, even in the movements of animals and the noises Ma made working in the kitchen.

James was asleep in our bed, but Annabel was helping Ma to mix up some batter. I walked back in and picked her up. I wanted to hold her and cry, but instead I twirled her round and round and laughed with her when she squealed, while Ma scolded us and shooed us away from her kitchen.

I went to Tennant's Rock at dusk that night, as I'd said. Ma didn't even ask where I was going, as if she were tired of questions and the kind of answers they always seemed to bring.

I sat on the rock in the gathering darkness, waiting as I had done that night in the forest when I came to look for Nate the first time, thinking he was camping out in the hills.

It was cold and there was a damp in the air that promised rain, but I waited until well after it was full dark and I was sure Nate wasn't going to make it.

As I walked home through the forest a fine, icy rain began to fall, blowing into my face and chilling me through. When I got back to the house Ma had coffee ready. She looked at me when she handed me a cup as I stood warming myself by the stove, but I just shook my head and looked away from her.

The next night I went again to Tennant's Rock. The weather had cleared after a day of showery rain and the air was sharp and cold. As darkness fell, a new moon appeared in the sky against a dust of cold bright stars. I was almost for going home again, my heart burning with the frustration of waiting, when I heard a horse down on the road beyond a belt of trees. Peering into the gloom I could see when Nate came out of the forest before he called out my name to reassure me it was him. Then he disappeared again around the far side of the scarp-shaped rock and I turned to see him climbing down toward me.

He sat down beside me and rubbed his hands for warmth.

'I thought we'd done with secret midnight meetings,' Nate said, and he made it into a joke but there was a question in there too.

'I waited last night, Nate, but I guess you couldn't come.'

'No.'

For a moment I thought he wasn't going to give me any explanation at all.

'I didn't get your note till I finished work and got back to the bunkhouse, maybe seven o'clock or later. I thought by the time I got here you'd be gone. I'd got, well I'd promised to do something for someone, couldn't get away.'

'That's all right, Nate, you're here now is the main thing,' and I put my hand on his.

'You know there's a lot of things I got to do before we set off for Oregon.'

'Sure.'

We sat in silence for a while, not an easy silence like we'd always seemed to have between us, but a silence of waiting. I was waiting for Nathan to ask me why I'd called him out there, but he didn't. I guess he knew I'd tell him when I was ready to, and I guess too he had a good idea of what it was I was going to say. So Nate was waiting, too.

'I think Ma would go along with you, Nate,' I told him at last, 'but I don't think it is right, what you're asking of her, I don't think it's right at all.'

'So that's it,' Nate said, 'Ma has decided I ain't going to get away with just a jail sentence.'

'I told you, Nate,' I said, feeling an anger rising in me that I wasn't used to, an anger that took me by surprise, 'Ma will go along with you. You can bring Marianne to the house Sunday and we will make her welcome and you will take her off to Oregon and she won't know a thing. But it ain't right, it ain't fair to Ma and it ain't fair to the woman you're going to marry.'

'Sissy, I spent the years I should've been growing into a man in jail. I had to do other men's work as well as my own, and steal and do other things, awful things, just to survive. Most of the men in there were big men, violent men, men who would do anything, Sissy, there wasn't nothing they wouldn't do to someone weaker than themselves.' His voice tailed away like he were choking on the memory of it.

'I've seen terrible things, Sissy, some things I've told you about and other things I couldn't begin to tell, not even to you, and I've done terrible things, too. Just to survive, Sissy, just so that I could get out of there one day and start my life

113

over. I want to be with someone doesn't know what I was, doesn't know nothing about Pa and prison, I want to leave all the past behind, Sissy, don't you understand that?'

I thought a moment, working something through my mind that I found difficult to believe.

'Are you telling me that Marianne don't know you've been to jail?'

Nate let out a sigh and said,

'Nobody knows who I am up there, Sissy, I don't use the name I had when I went to jail, you know that, I don't let it be known that I come from these parts. Aside from Mr Packer and one other friend of mine, a good friend, no-one knows where I'm really from, that I was ever in jail, that I killed a man. All the neighbours between here and the Turner place have moved on, and I don't look nothing like the boy they sent to jail.'

'But you've told her, you've told Marianne that you got a Ma and sister living nearby?'

'Sure I've told her. I wanted to bring her over to see you, to see my folks.'

'Doesn't she wonder why no-one else knows about us?'

'Well, yes,' he hesitated a moment, then went on, speaking fast,

'But I told her I didn't want nobody to know who or where I was, and I give her a reason for that, she don't need to know about me and Pa just because of that.'

'What did you tell her, Nate?'

Nate was quiet again, I knew he wouldn't answer me and I knew why. I didn't want to hear him say it, but I had to know for sure.

'Was it some lie about us, Nate?'

'Not about you, Sissy, nor Ma.'

'Pa then?'

Nate didn't answer.

'Did you tell her something about Pa, Nate, some lie about him?'

'He's dead, Sissy, nothing I say can hurt him now.'

I felt sick, a pain inside my stomach like I'd eaten something bad. I could feel fear in Nate, some kind of defiance that I couldn't understand, and that falling again, falling endlessly into darkness.

'Don't you think she's strong enough, that she loves you enough, to know the truth about you?' I asked him.

'It ain't the truth, Sissy, I ain't no murderer. What happened to Pa was an accident.'

I turned to him again and put my hand on his arm. I felt a great tenderness for him, but I knew that something had changed between us, that there was nothing more that we could do for each other, and I knew what it was that I'd always been able to feel around him, that I could feel when he appeared at our door that day, that mean dog that followed Nate around, that thing that made him run from his guilt and run from Swann, that was making him now build a new life on a lie, and would, I thought, chase him away from that in the end, unless he turned on it now, fought it now, ran it off his heels.

'Tell her, Nate,' I said, 'ride on back now, see her in the morning before you both start work, tell her, please.'

The urgency and pleading in my voice made him stop. I could feel the confusion in his thoughts, the fear in him. He waited, trying to find some courage in his heart that just wasn't there.

'I can't, Sissy,' was all he said.

'Then you killed Pa twice over,' I told him, and I pulled myself up too quick from the rocks, feeling the sharp edges tug and tear at the good stuff of my winter dress, and moved away from him, scrambling and jumping up from the bank.

I expected Nate to follow or at least cry out after me, but

all I heard was a noise like a child makes when it is hungry or hurt and too tired to know its own thoughts, and when I turned round to look Nate was holding his head in his hands and sobbing and crying into them. My flesh ached to go back to him but I thought of Ma and of the daughter she would have, the woman wed in a lie to her only son, and I knew that there was nothing more to be said between us, that the time for gentle words had passed.

11

Pete Anderson

I hadn't said nothing to Ma about the bad feeling that had come between Nate and me on our last meeting. I cried a little to myself at night, but that wasn't nothing I hadn't done before. Nate had let me down, but I was growed enough to know that what had happened had to be lived with. I'd wanted Nate to come home, to help work the farm, to make sure we had no more of Swann or others like him, to share the love that Ma and me and Annabel and James could make happen. I wanted us to be a family again, like I thought I remembered us being, though Nate didn't remember it that way.

When I knew Nate wasn't coming home I was happy for him but the pain inside was almost too much to bear. Now I knew how weak he was, how we never would be able to trust or rely on him, the pain was bigger but somehow I could stand it better. I found inside myself a kind of courage I hadn't thought to need. I was determined not to go the way Nate had gone. I was going to meet my new sister and maybe, even though she would be clear away to Oregon, maybe sometime in the future she would need me to help her through the bad times that I knew would come to her because of Nate. I was not going to let him come between us.

There was the wedding, too, with music and dancing and fancy clothes I'd never seen and wanted so much to see now, even if the idea scared me more than anything I could think of. So I put on all my smiles and closed off the bad feelings inside me, let the excitement grow in me, partly so's I could fool Ma and partly so's I could fool myself. And all the time I knew, I guess, that Ma was doing just exactly the same, but instead of smiles and excitement she put on this calm and dignity like she would put on a shawl.

We spent Saturday cleaning and scrubbing twice over, things Ma scrubbed most every day anyway. We put the children to bed early so they couldn't mess things up, then turned them out into the yard with a hunk of cornbread for breakfast as soon as they woke.

Winter was truly over at last and everything between the house and the river was glowing bright with warm sunlight. I thought how Nate had said Marianne's hair was golden and how the bright sunshine would catch it, making her into that painting or poem of day that he'd seen in her. That morning it didn't seem to matter that Nate had hurt me so, I didn't have to fight no more to forget, I was just filled up with joy and longing to see her, to look at this sister that I knew now, though I'd never given it a thought, I'd always felt the lack of like a wound.

And while we sat waiting for them to arrive, scared to move in case I messed up the perfect bright cleanness of everything around me, things would come into my mind, new things I hadn't thought before, things that made me fill up with warmth, made me smile, made me near cry out for joy at it all.

I picked up a book Nate had given me, I think it was the first I ever read without pictures, and I thought how if Nate wanted Marianne for his wife she must be learned in reading and writing, and how even though she would be far away we would be able to write each other letters.

And I thought how smart Nate was, and how sure I was that their farm would prosper and that they would get rich, rich enough to travel down from Oregon some times and see us, they would have children who would call me Aunt Sissy, just like Annabel and James said Uncle Nate. Maybe some day soon the railroad would reach from here to there and we could all visit.

I tried to imagine sitting on a railroad train with Annabel growed up, maybe her own baby on her knee, and there was James growed into a man in a collar and necktie, reading a book, but my head swam with it and though I'd seen a picture of a railroad train and knew what it looked like, I didn't know at all what happened inside them, what they were like to look at in the part where folks sat to ride from place to place.

Noon came and there was no sign of Nate. Ma had two young chickens roasting in the stove and the smell made my mouth water. The children were restless and excited too, knowing they were going to meet a brand new aunt, that Nate would bring them a present, that they were going to have roast chicken and a big pudding with dried fruit in it and real sugar Grandma had bought from the trading boat. Everything was set.

When I heard the horse's hooves coming towards us my heart leapt again, I felt that keen happiness that comes when frustration is broken and ends, when waiting is over and what has been waited on arrives. But the feeling lasted only a moment before I knew that something wasn't right, that there was only one horse, no cart nor carriage, and that Nate would surely not bring his intended to see us riding on the back of his horse, twenty or more miles across open country and rutted, half-made roads. The horse I could hear was riding hard, it was ridden by a man alone, not one lingering through a Sabbath with his sweetheart.

It was the same boy had brought Nate's letter a few days earlier, though I hardly recognised him. He had put on a smart grey Sabbath suit and a pale-coloured hat tied under his chin as if he wasn't used to it. He looked older, maybe as old as me, almost as much of a man as Nate.

He nodded toward me and dismounted. Annabel and James moved close to me and stared up at him. Ma, realising it wasn't Nate arriving, came out of the house behind me and watched. I could feel her there and see her out of the corner of my eye, I wanted to turn to see the expression on her face, but didn't want either to take my eyes off the boy who stood in front of me, now removing his hat and holding it nervously in his hand, toying with it the way I have seen men do since in front of ladies they don't know but wish to speak with. When he took off his hat you could see that he had oiled his hair and combed it back over his head so that it covered his neck and hung down over his collar.

He looked at me and past me at Ma. He nodded and swallowed, all the boyish confidence of his previous visit seemed to have ebbed away.

'Ma'am,' was all he could manage to say. I nodded back at him, tried a smile.

He began to talk again but stammered over his words so that they came out at first without any sense to them. I couldn't understand what had caused the change in him. Eventually he managed to tell us what was obvious enough, that he had come from Nate, that he had brought word from him that the visit would have to be delayed.

'Is Nathan's fiancée sick?' I asked him.

For a moment he looked alarmed, then he stammered out,

120

'Yes, ma'am, she's just got a little sickness to the stomach, Miss Henry that is, that Nate is to marry, and she sends her apologies and compliments . . . ' he stammered badly over compliments, as if he were reading and found the longer words difficult, 'and hopes to see you next Sabbath.'

'I hope she'll be all right.'

The boy nodded again, just as nervously, and said he was sure she would be. He seemed to want to be away, and though I felt sorry for him I wasn't anxious to delay him. I was relieved by what he told me, relieved not to have to wait any more and to be given a simple explanation of why Nate was not coming. Disappointment filled me, I felt almost that I wanted to cry, but I told myself this was foolish and that I could wait another week for the sister I'd waited near nineteen years for.

I thanked the boy, wondered whether I should offer him some food, then Ma's voice behind me said,

'Well we ain't going to leave you standing there hungry on a Sabbath or any other day, when we've food for more than we need ready to lay on the table.'

I turned to Ma, a little surprised, I guess, and I could feel in her a bitterness that was more than a disappointment that Nate hadn't come that day. Till I looked into her face I felt nothing beyond that, had no doubts that the reason Nate had given for not bringing Marianne to see us was true. There was some deep hurt there in Ma's face that I couldn't understand, that I felt then was unfair to Nate, that even though my faith in him had gone I did not think he deserved his mother's scorn to be written so bold on her.

I turned back to the boy, who hesitated, as if he for some reason perceived me to be the mistress of the house and could not accept an invitation until I had delivered it.

'What do they call you?' I asked him right out, having no experience of talking to strangers.

He grinned and made that little gesture again, more of a duck of the head than a nod, and his large Adam's apple moved down his throat as he swallowed dry.

'Anderson, ma'am,' he said, the grin disappearing from his face as suddenly and inexplicably as it had arrived, 'Pete Anderson.'

'Well, Mr Anderson, if you want to go indoors with Mrs Holt, I'll see to your horse.'

And that's what I did, the children following me close, watching my movements and keeping a frightened eye on the house to see if the mysterious stranger, who for some reason was not Uncle Nate and had brought with him no fine lady and no gifts, would emerge to do them some harm.

Mr Anderson proved more than a match for the mountains of food Ma and me had prepared. As she said after, it was a treat and fascination to watch him do justice to our cooking.

At first, not being used to having a stranger to dinner – I couldn't ever recall it happening before – there wasn't much talk. But Mr Anderson it seemed, when he got over his fear of us, was the talking kind, and when Ma asked him a question, me being of a sudden mostly too shy to, he answered her with long stories about his life, what he'd heard about this or that, his views on farming and the weather and things in general, and most anything else that came into his head. All the time he grew in confidence, I felt like I was watching him grow into manhood right there in front of me at the Sabbath table.

'How old are you, Mr Anderson?' Ma asked, and he told her he was seventeen.

'Well, well. Mrs Swann here is seventeen, ain't you?'

'Eighteen, Ma,' I told her, startled first of all because she had given something away about me, my age, and because she'd called me Mrs Swann, which I didn't remember being called before.

The name, and the presence of the children, obviously seemed to Ma to require some explanation.

'Oh,' she started, as if Mr Anderson had enquired after my husband, 'she had a man but he weren't no good.' She sighed, as if at the ways of the world or of men, and said, 'Now he's gone away for good,' in a tone which implied that this was a matter of great regret to us both. Then she dropped the subject, and we ate in silence for a while until she turned to Mr Anderson again and said,

'You always lived in these parts?'

'Yes, ma'am,' he said, politely emptying his mouth before speaking.

'Folks live round here too?'

'Well, they did, but I ain't got no folks no more. Ma died when I was around six years old and Pa took off.'

'What come of him?'

'I don't know, ma'am. He just took hisself off one day.'

'Leave you all alone without a word?'

'No, ma'am, took me to a old woman down to Colusa, but she treated me worse'n a dog, so when I got growed, to around nine or ten I guess, I took off from there. Ma'am,' he said, eying the dish of potatoes in the middle of the table, 'I don't believe I ever tasted anything as good as this before.'

Ma smiled and shook her head, spooned the rest of the potatoes on to his plate and passed the gravy over to him. Seeing the empty dish, James started to demand more potatoes too, even though he hardly ate enough to keep a flea hopping, as Ma always said, and had almost all the food I'd given him either still on his plate or in his hair. I lifted him on to my knee and began to spoon his food into his mouth, in big enough mouthfuls to keep him quiet.

'What you do then?' Ma asked Mr Anderson, when the commotion had subsided.

'Went on over to Eureka,' he answered, 'didn't know what went on up there but I had a hankering, don't know where it come from, to see the ocean. Some miners there didn't have no womenfolk, took me in if I could work, I done cooked for them, sewed. That old woman taught me stuff, I will say.'

'They treat you mean?'

'No, ma'am, they treat me fair, fed me, gave me a little change, treat me like I was their boy.'

'Why d'you leave?'

James was trying to wriggle away from me and I decided to let him go. He toddled off around the edge of the table. I nodded to Annabel, who knew that meant to keep her eye on him, young as she was. I was enjoying listening to Mr Anderson's life story, and didn't want to have to break off.

'Wanted to see more of life, I guess,' he went on. 'I got to growing up and didn't want to work them mines, always liked the idea of farming, so thought I'd come back to the Sacramento Valley. Anyway, my best friend there, they called him Tim Sykes, he took a knife in the belly one night in a fight over a – that is, in a fight, ma'am – and he died. So I didn't really feel like that was my home no more.'

'So now you work for Mr Turner?'

James was getting too near the stove, but Ma had stood up to bring the bowls of boiled almond pudding that would serve for dessert, and she lifted him away.

'Yes, ma'am,' Mr Anderson said, gazing at the pudding like it had been a bag of gold nuggets, 'but someday I'd like my own place, you know, like Nate is getting up there in Oregon.'

'Well, you work real hard and you'll have it.'

'Yes, ma'am.'

Ma took all this in her stride, having seen some of the world herself, but to me, who'd hardly left the farm where I was born, it sounded as exotic as the stories in the books that Nate brought for me. I wanted to hear more, but after my boldness in asking his name, I could hardly bring myself to talk at all. I could not remember hearing Ma talk this way, though I suppose she'd never really had the opportunity. She just seemed to take to Pete Anderson and once she'd taken to him, to open out a whole side of herself that had been hid for years.

The children, too, were soon won over. They had been expecting a party, and though Uncle Nate let them down, Mr Anderson did not. Having been a kind of mascot to those miners, he could easily rival Nate for tricks and stunts to keep the two of them amused. He built a dart out of a sheet of paper and made it fly across the room. He made a penny disappear, found it behind Annabel's ear, then endeared hisself to her by letting her keep the penny. He said to Ma,

'You got a dog round here I can use to show this lady and gentleman something real funny?'

Both Ma and me must have shown something in our faces because he said, quick,

'Don't worry, I won't hurt him none, it's just an old trick I can teach him if he ain't the kind bites anybody he ain't acquainted to.'

Ma said,

'We ain't got no dog, now, we had one but he died and we never got around to replacing him, I guess.'

'Lord, ma'am,' he said, shaking his head, 'you ain't got

no menfolks here you should get yourselves a dog. Anyway, farm ain't a farm without one. I bet Annabel here would like a dog wouldn't you, Annabel?'

Annabel stared up at him. She was almost six but she hadn't once been off the farm, Pirate had died while I was carrying her, and she'd never seen a dog in her life, unless you count the ones in the picture books Nate brought for us.

Ma insisted on doing all the planting that week, even though we hadn't heard from Nate. It was hard work for two women, but Ma had done it alone in the past and said it wouldn't wait. We got it done, though it wore us out.

The following Saturday and Sabbath we repeated the whole performance of cleaning and waiting, but Nate did not arrive. We sat as we had the week before, the children playing in the yard in the warm spring sunshine. Ma waited until an hour or so after noon then began to serve the food.

'Don't you think we ought to wait a little longer?' I asked Ma. 'Maybe they got held up.'

She looked at me, put down a ladle she was holding.

'He ain't coming, Sissy,' she said.

There was a silence between us, a silence that truth seemed somehow to pour into like rain water into an empty bucket.

'How do you know, Ma?' I asked her. She didn't answer, but picked up the ladle again and moved toward the stove.

'How do you know he ain't coming?' There was an urgency in my voice that made her stop and turn back to me. Her eyes narrowed and she looked away, then back at me. She seemed to stand in that silence looking at me through her narrowed eyes for a long, long time. When finally she spoke her voice was quiet.

'He's my son, ain't he?' was all she said.

We ate in silence. Even James made hardly a sound. When Annabel asked Ma where Uncle Nate was she said,

'He ain't coming.'

'Will he come next week?'

'No, child.'

'You don't know that, Ma,' I said, but I didn't believe it.

For the second Sabbath in a row we ate roast chicken with good gravy, greens and sweet potatoes. I knew that Nate lacked not only courage but trust, that he had failed me so badly that nothing would ever be the same again. If I was to meet my new sister now, if I was to see her before Nate took her off to Oregon, then I would have to leave the farm, to ride all alone to the Turner ranch, ask questions and favours of strangers. My heart raced and my stomach heaved at the thought of it, but I knew that I had to do it. I had seen at such a tender age the evil of strength and the wickedness of weakness, and I did not envy Marianne her lot. She would need me in Oregon, and if only she knew how to write, as surely any bride of Nate's would, then she would have a sister to turn to when Nate betrayed her, as I knew some day he must.

12

Nate's Wedding

I set out early next morning, took the horse and buggy. Ma knew where I was going, and I had to promise to be back before nightfall. I took some food, and a shotgun.

It didn't take too long to find the Turner place. It was a ranch that stretched further than the eye could see, and once on it you could follow a good, well kept road to the big white house where Mr Turner lived with his family. I recognised it all from Nate's description, even saw the bunkhouse where he and the other hands slept.

I had put on my best dress, not the one Ma was making me for the wedding, that was still not finished, but one I'd bought ready sewn from Mrs Packer on the trading boat, that she said had come from a fine lady in Sacramento who had decided she didn't have no more use for it. It was grey with white trims, warm and respectable without making me look too much the farm girl I was.

I left the buggy by the porch and walked up to the big wooden door. I was scared enough to turn around and run, but I knew I mustn't. The door had a big brass ring in it and the ring sat in the mouth of what I took for a big dog, till I remembered seeing the picture of the lion in a book of bible stories. Recalling the story of Daniel made me draw up some courage, and I lifted up the heavy brass ring and let it fall against the door. Nothing happened for what seemed an age, and I was about to lift up the knocker again when I heard footsteps inside and the door opened.

I'd never seen a coloured person before, nor much of anyone else if it came to that, and I guess I must have stared. I didn't make too good a start, anyway, and when the maid got through staring at me staring at her, her voice sounded unfriendly and suspicious. All my fear came back. I wanted to cry, I wanted to lean my head on this tall young woman's shoulder and have her hold me and comfort me, but at the same time I was frightened even to open my mouth to her. Mr Anderson had made me nervous enough, but at least when I met him he had been on my land, in my home. This woman, standing in front of and above me, looking down her nose with an expression of suspicion and disdain, was at home, and she was the first stranger I'd met away from the farm since I'd been a little child.

I finally found my voice.

'Excuse me,' I said, politely as Ma had taught me, 'I'm looking for one of the hands works for Mr Turner here.'

'There's a lot of hands here, lady.' She said it like she wanted to be rid of me, all the time standing and holding the door by its edge, ready as it seemed to close it at any moment.

'He goes by the name of Nate, or Nathan.'

She looked surprised and took me in once more as she had when she first opened the door, her eyes measuring my length up and down.

'Nate Page?' The name Nate had invented for hisself sounded strange spoke out loud, but I'd wrote to him under it and I knew what to expect.

I nodded. The woman smiled, not unkindly but not in a way which showed warming toward me neither.

'Wait there,' she said, and closed the door.

A few minutes later I heard footsteps again and the door opened. This time a very grand-looking, middle-aged white lady appeared, though I could see the maid hovering around in the background.

I found myself bobbing my head and swallowing into a dry throat, just like Pete Anderson had when he talked to me and Ma in our yard the week before. The woman looked me up and down, more openly than the maid had done.

'Mrs Turner?' I asked. She laughed.

'No, child, Mr and Mrs Turner are away right now. I'm in charge of the house, though. Did Nate tell you to come here?'

My heart rose when she said this, and for a moment I thought I could see the explanation for what had happened. Maybe Mr Turner had taken Nate with him wherever he'd gone, and Nate hadn't been able to get in touch. Maybe the boat would bring a letter on Wednesday. I felt foolish to be there at all.

'No, ma'am,' I answered her.

She looked puzzled and said,

'Well, no matter. You got any experience this kind of work?'

I froze, not knowing what to say to her, not knowing at all what she was asking me. I felt my head shake from side to side, and heard her begin to say something about how Mrs Turner was really looking for someone who had worked as a lady's maid before. I had to force myself to speak.

'I'm sorry,' I managed to say, 'I'm not looking for work, that isn't why I'm here.'

The housekeeper stopped and looked at me curiously. Behind her the maid was pretending to sweep the wide staircase that began a few yards beyond the door, but I could feel her listening.

130

'You see, I'm Mr Page's sister, and I'd like to see him if I could. I know he's likely—'

The woman interrupted me, still with her puzzled expression.

'I'm sorry, miss,' she said, 'but Nate left here straight after his wedding. Him and Marianne, that is I should say him and Mrs Page, have set off for Oregon. You see, that's why Mrs Turner is looking out for a new girl.'

I knew then just what Nate had done. I knew at last how much he could do, knew that Ma had been right. There was no anger in me, only some great sadness that he had thought he had to rob me of a sister to keep a wife. I apologised and turned to walk away. For some reason I stopped at the edge of the porch and, holding myself as best I could I said,

'Is Mr Anderson around?'

The housekeeper looked surprised, then smiled.

'Pete? No, miss, he ain't. Pete had to go on down to Marysville the beginning of last week and he ain't got back.' She moved nearer. 'To tell you the truth, him and Nate been friends ever since Nate first come here but I think they had some kind of bust-up, and Pete made sure he wasn't here for the wedding. Maybe Pete had his eye on Marianne, too.'

She laughed, but she must have read some distress in my face that made her add, kindly,

'Don't worry, honey, I guess you and Nate must have gotten the dates mixed around or something.'

As I rode away I felt a strange light-headedness, as if I'd shaken off that precious, burdensome thing that Nate had given me when he talked about my beauty and his love. I thought how strange that I should feel the loss of a sister I'd never known more than that of a brother that I'd loved, that I still loved. I wondered, for a moment, what Nate had told her about us, how he had explained to her that we wouldn't be at the wedding. I knew, too, that Nate had thrown away a friend as well as his sister and his mother, that Pete Anderson had known of his secret and that Nate's intention not to tell Marianne the truth was what had caused their quarrel.

About halfway home I stopped by the banks of a stream to eat the food Ma had packed for me, but it stuck in my mouth, dry and tasteless, and wouldn't wash down with the sweet water from the brook. I cried then, but when I found I could stop I promised myself it would be the last time and that Nate, like Swann before him, had had his share of my tears.

13

Ma

'I knew all the time that that was what Nate was planning' was what Ma said when I told her. 'Least, I knew it after that second time he didn't show up. But there wasn't no use in telling you that, Sissy, so I thought I'd let you ride over there and see for yourself, even though I knew it would break your heart to do it.'

She was standing on the porch and looked away from me, over to the field and the edge of the forest, almost like she was scanning the horizon for someone she expected any time to see.

'Maybe Nathan was right to do it that way, I don't know.' She sounded weary.

I was surprised, expected her to be angry, like I'd seen her before, like I knew she was when we got Nate's letter.

'It ain't right to lie to his wife that way, Ma, and it ain't right to lie to us neither,' I told her.

'No, Sissy, it ain't. But he's done like I told him, gone on up to Oregon to forget the past. What he done is done, and there wasn't no sense pretending we could ever be a real family again. Maybe he'll tell her, in his own good time.'

'I thought I was going to have a sister, Ma,' I said, and wished I'd bit off my tongue rather than said it. But Ma just looked at me and shook her head a little. She reached out her hand to me, and took hold of mine. She looked into my face and said, softly,

'I'd've give you one if I could, Sissy.'

I smiled now, looked at her face in the sunlight. She was starting to look her age, with the work we had now we were left to fend for ourselves again, but there was no weakness or defeat about her.

'You know I didn't mean nothing, Ma,' I said.

It was coming on evening now, and we broke the awkward silence that came from Ma's thoughts by rounding up the children and putting them to bed. James hadn't liked me leaving him all day, but he must have worn hisself out with his anger at it, because both of them fell asleep almost as soon as I got them into bed. Ma lit the lamp and we sat at the table. I could tell she wanted to talk some more, that there was something in her mind had to be put into words.

'Nate ain't got so far to go,' Ma said at last, leaning back in her chair, 'but they will have to get past some Indians ain't always awful glad to see white faces. I guess Nate remembers enough about life on the trail to know what he is letting his wife in for.'

It was strange now, when Nate had finally hurt me so badly, to hear Ma talk of him as she might of any son. I watched her, watched her mind wandering over the tracks and trails of her past.

'You know,' she said after a while, 'I never did want to leave Ohio, we had a good farm and good neighbours and a life of plenty, but your Pa had this idea, he wanted his life to be an adventure, you see, so many of the men were that way, that is how they saw things, and us women just had to tag along. All the time we was getting ready to leave, sewing up clothes and wagon covers. For weeks before we went friends and neighbours would come around, always the womenfolk come to see our women, the men didn't seem to mind it somehow. They only had their eyes on where we was going. And every one of our friends would leave us in tears.

'We had no idea what it was going to be like. We left Independence with the wagons all looking so spruce, all the women in good dresses, it looked like Sabbath. I done our wagon up just like home, made pockets on the inside of the cloth lining to keep things in, kept my own things in there, a looking glass even, combs and things, as if you could carry on being the fine lady out there on the trail. Many a morning I cursed that looking glass for showing me what I'd become.' And Ma laughed.

'Clothes just got wore out and by the time we'd been a month on the trail we was all in rags. I had a good dress caught fire when I was cooking, and your Pa wrapped me in a Indian blanket to put out the flames. I didn't get burned hardly at all, but the dress was gone and I cried and cried over it. Your Grandma had made it for me, and I knew I'd never see her again.'

Ma paused, and I saw the cloud of sadness at the loss, one of so many in her life, pass across her eyes. Then they brightened, and she shook her head.

'Then one time we nearly lost Nate,' she said. 'The wagon was forcing its way through this pass all strewn with rocks, Nate was eight or nine, leaning out the back the way boys will, pointing up in the sky with a stick he was making believe for a rifle, and out he went. I couldn't believe how he survived with just a scratch, no broken bones nor cuts to speak of.'

Ma went quiet, thinking of Nate I guess, and in the dim light I thought she must have dozed off. I couldn't let her sleep there in the chair so I said,

'Ma,' softly, to wake her gently, but she wasn't asleep at all.

'What is it, Sissy?' she asked, not like a person coming out of sleep but as one being pulled from a daydream.

'You ain't never told me much about the trail before, Ma,' I said.

'There never seemed time, child. We ain't never been left in peace to talk such things over, but maybe now we will be, maybe now.'

She lapsed again into silence. Suddenly she said,

'You know, Sissy, I still don't wish we'd stayed back in Ohio, even after all that's happened. Ain't no saying what would've happened if we'd stayed, and if I lost my man for coming out west, I learnt enough on that trail to help me fend without him.' She paused, went on,

'I don't mean to make it sound like I ever got over your Pa dying that way, Sissy,' she said. 'I don't believe I would've gotten over it however he was taken from me. Some things you can't never make up for. But when I was on that trail we women had to be women and men both. We loaded up those wagons, we drove them, we helped out with the cattle. And I think it's on account of that that I can take my daughter into the field and we can plant out our seed, make as sure as the Lord permits we'll have plenty to eat come fall, and not have to beg or pay some man to do it for us. And pretty soon I'll be taking my granddaughter out there too. Man's a useful thing, but he ain't worth any price.'

I thought about Swann, and the price I'd paid for him, but I didn't say nothing.

'If I'd been younger,' Ma went on, maybe seeing my thoughts, 'we could've dug that cellar without Swann. We can sure enough manage the ploughing and the planting and the reaping on our own, Sissy. Ain't no work I ever seen as hard as washing day, anyway.' And Ma laughed to herself, recalling, or so it felt to me, times long past.

'Now we're going to get by just fine,' she went on, her

voice growing excited. 'We got all we need to make butter and cheese to sell to Mr Packer, and that'll sure make it easier to get by.' Again she lapsed into the silence of her thoughts.

'I don't blame nobody for it, Sissy, but there was times on that trail, when you was coming, I never want to know pain like that again. The worst of it was, we couldn't stop for so long, not until you was well on your way. There was folks there didn't like to travel on the Sabbath, but we had to keep right on going no matter what.

'It wouldn't have been so bad if you'd come along sooner. When we first set out there was plenty of womenfolk and we would sustain each other through the bad times, we'd visit each other like our wagons was real homes, we'd walk along together and talk over old times, we'd help each other out with problems we had, things we needed to get by. But most of our party was headed for Idaho and Wyoming. I wanted to head there too but there wasn't no point in going against your Pa, him and some of the other men were set on California and gold, so that's where we were going. But he was the only married one amongst 'em. So by the time you come along I was the only female in the camp and I had a hard time of it.'

She laughed, quietly, and shook her head.

'Course when I reached the end of my confinement they couldn't do nothing 'cept run around like chickens playing host to a hungry fox. Your Pa rode up ahead twenty miles and when he come back he said there was a lady on the way would help me.

'I never will forget her, though I never saw her before or since. All I knew was she was called Mrs Jonson or Johnstone, spoke with a strange kind of accent, she must've been fifty years old but she had the most beautiful blonde hair tied up in a way I hadn't seen before, like a bun right on the top of her head. As soon as she arrived she calmed me, her hands on me were like whisky on a toothache, and she brought you out like she done it every day. Then she just rode off and I never saw her again, but I sure hope she prospered out here.'

In the night, with Ma's sweet voice talking over the small hiss of the lamp and the sound of the crickets out beyond the cabin, I felt more at peace than I had at any time since Pa had died. I was sleepy, but I wanted Ma to go on talking all night.

'Did the men treat you bad, Ma, when you was the only woman? Did you have to do all the women's work yourself while you was carrying and nursing me?' I asked her.

She smiled at that.

'Well, they worked me awful hard, it's true. But they helped me some, too, and then maybe they thought more of me because they didn't have no others. They always tried to find me wood if they could,' she laughed, 'cause if they couldn't I had to cook on that buffalo dirt, and I never did like to have to do that, or to eat the food had been cooked on it. Not that it tasted any different, I suppose, but I just never liked the idea of it.'

We both smiled at that.

'And I always had the last word about where we would camp,' Ma said. 'We heard stories about women going crazy and taking a horsewhip to their husbands, setting light to their wagons, running off on their own into the mountains and never being heard of again, all kinds of things. What scared 'em most though was when I threatened to pour away the last of the barrel of whisky after a couple of them got good and drunk one night. We never should have been carrying it anyhow, when we had to throw things away were more needed, so we could get over those mountain trails. Your Pa threatened to sell me to an Indian if I done that, and I told him I'd run off with the first one I saw if he didn't make sure there weren't no more drinking and the whisky was saved for when it was needed to kill pain. Funny thing is, he never cared for whisky anyway, but it was like he had to stand up to me in front of the other men. It started out with a joke about the Indian, but it got into the worst fight we ever had, and I cried and cried all night after it.

'Then things got better, maybe because they were afraid I was going crazy, like I said. They always let me choose the camping place, and I made them burn the grass there to keep off snakes and crawling things before we all bedded down. There was always some would help with the cooking, too. And we all made it to California, Sissy, we made it through those deserts and over those mountains and past Indians and wild beasts and here we are.'

It was round then that a mountain lion got in amongst our chickens. Late one night we heard the commotion the hens made when she got in amongst them, Ma was up before me, rifle in her hand, out the door of the cabin before I was even full awake.

My first thought was that Swann had come back, then that a grizzly was maybe trying to force his way in, though I'd never known such a thing happen before. While all this was running through my mind I didn't want to leave James and Annabel, who slept sound through the whole thing, so I stood by their bed with the shotgun in my hand, my eyes fixed on the door Ma had left swinging open in the breeze. But when I heard the shot I ran to the door to make sure Ma was safe.

I couldn't see nothing at all at first, just the empty yard and the night shapes around it, and I wouldn't leave my babies alone there, not even for Ma. Then I saw her come walking back toward me, still holding her rifle, and I called to her.

'It's all right now, child,' she said, 'I seen it off, though I don't think I hit it.'

She lit a lamp and told me about the mountain lion.

'Must've scratched her way in underneath. I hope we got some chickens left.'

The damage looked worse than it was. There was blood and feathers all around the coop, but when we counted up only four hens were missing, two of them laying more or less intact on the floor and one she must've carried off, the other accounting for most of the mess.

We cleaned up the dirt and mess as best we could, and left the damage until daybreak to repair, but we didn't go back to bed. Ma made some coffee and we sat up and waited for first light, Ma with her rifle across her lap. We didn't talk much. Ma looked out in front of her, busy with her thoughts, and I read a book and dozed a little. Once Ma laughed softly to herself and I smiled and asked,

'What is it?'

She shook her head and looked at me.

'I was just thinking of you with that shotgun by the door. You'd let her off in the hen house you'd have scared the lion well enough, but there'd have been more dead chickens than she could've killed if we'd left her there till sunrise.'

'But Ma, I wouldn't have done that, I thought you'd gone out there chasing grizzlies,' and we both laughed at that, laughed so much we heard James stir in his sleep and had to hold our hands over our mouths for fear of waking him.

14

Dreams and Memories

I was standing on the porch of the Turner place, waiting for the maid to come back to tell me if Nate and Marianne had returned from Oregon. The door opened and a fine lady in a long white dress stood looking at me. I started to speak but she held up her hand and motioned me through the door.

The same maid who had answered the door on my first visit was standing at the bottom of the stairs. She smiled when she saw me and stepped close, putting her arms around me and kissing me on the forehead. I felt warm and safe in her arms, and the closeness of her body and the comfort of it made me feel weak and shaky inside myself. I felt I could have stood there snuggled inside her, leaning against her strong, tall body for ever, but after a while she let me go, still smiling, squeezed my hand and tripped lightly off through a big door to one side of the hallway.

I looked around for the other woman, and saw her at the top of the wide staircase in front of me. I followed her up, feeling happier than I could ever remember feeling, but when I got to the top she had disappeared.

I walked along a corridor toward an open door, through which I could hear the sounds of a crowd of people in high spirits. I passed through the door and found myself in a room with maybe fifteen or twenty people. James and Annabel were there, dressed in fine clothes and eating pastries and sweets from a long table at one end of the room. When they saw me they waved and shouted, 'Hello, Mamma.' Ma was standing near to them, and she waved too.

Then I saw Nate, standing with a tall, fair woman who I knew straight away was Marianne. She was wearing a bridal dress and veil, though the veil was turned back from her face and I thought she was the most beautiful thing I'd ever seen. When I looked at her I had that same feeling of weakness and warmth and safety I had when the maid had held me in her arms downstairs. I wanted to walk over to them both, they were smiling at me and waiting for me to approach, but all at once there seemed far more people in the room than there had been when I first arrived, and I couldn't see a way through to them. I tried to push my way round the edge of the room, losing sight of them as I did so. As I moved through the crowded room I saw more people that I knew, Mr and Mrs Packer, Pete Anderson, even a man who'd come round to the farm a few years before repairing shoes. I saw the maid again, too, and the housekeeper. But I couldn't see Nate or Marianne no more, nor Annabel or James or Ma.

I started to feel a little uneasy, the crowd seemed to push in on me and the room felt hot. I saw an open door opposite the one I'd come in through and made for it. By the time I got to it the room was so crowded that I had to squeeze out of the press into the space beyond the door. I found myself in a small, empty room, painted white. Opposite me was another door.

I took a few steps toward the door and felt a sudden fear in my stomach. I stopped, and tried to turn back to rejoin the safety of the party, but when I looked behind me there was no door where I thought it had been, only bare white wall. I took another step, then stopped short, frozen still with terror. There was nothing I could see, but I could feel the fear blazing through the open door like a light, hear a laboured, heavy breathing, a shuffling of something heavy across the floor. I tried to scream, but all I could hear coming from my mouth was a loud moan, deep and pitiful, that frightened Annabel lying in the bed beside me so we had to hold each other tight.

There is no better thing to chase out fear than the fear your children feel and the need they have of your strength when they feel it.

I had this same dream over and over after Nate left, not always exactly like this but always the same in some ways. There was a strong-looking woman to hold me like the maid did, a room full of people, happy and friendly, a cold, white, empty room beyond that and beyond that a nameless terror that I felt and usually heard but woke before I saw it.

I missed Nate bad, missed his letters and our meetings by the river. I remembered how he would read to me from his favourite books, *Uncle Tom's Cabin* and *Ivanhoe* and *Deerslayer* and *Twice-Told Tales*. Sometimes he would tell me stories he had heard from the other hands, tales of the adventures they'd had drifting around the west, funny stories about farmers who couldn't farm, chickens tricking foxes out of eating them, people being swindled by their own greed. He told me about politics, too, and that as far as he could see ladies ought to be able to vote just the same as men.

'But, Nate,' I told him, 'I wouldn't know who to vote for.'

'Well, Sissy,' he said, putting on one of the voices he liked to do, 'you got the choice, you could either vote for the party that saved the Union or the one that durned near destroyed it. You hear about the young feller on a farm just by here?'

I shook my head, knowing I was in for one of Nate's tall stories.

'And come election time this here Democrat feller rides up on his fine horse and he says, Good Morning, young man, are you old enough to vote? And the young feller tells him he guesses he is. So this Democrat there says to him, Well, I'm here to ask you to cast your vote for Mr Swindlebags, who's your candidate for the great Democratic party. And the young feller says he thanks him kindly but he didn't think he could do that, cause he intended to vote the Republican ticket. May I ask why? says the Democrat. Well, says the young feller, You see my Grandpa and my Pa and my older brother and all my uncles have voted the Republican ticket straight through since '56, and I ain't got a mind to go against them. Well, says the Democrat, thinking he's got the young feller where he wants him, What would you do if your Grandpa and Pa and brother and uncles had all been durned fools? Then, says the young feller, chewing on his piece of straw, I guess I'd vote Democrat.'

When Nate told a story like this he would roar with laughter, so that even if I didn't understand it or find it amusing I would catch it and have to laugh with him. Other times he would make me laugh by clowning around, like the time he showed me how he practised his wrassling all on his own, reaching an arm around his head and pretending to pull hisself over by his nose. If it was warm he would always manage to fall in the river somehow, then pretend a crocodile had got his leg or some other foolery. He would tell me things, crazy things I'd either believe or half-believe, being so young and having had so little experience of the world.

Once he told me his horse could talk and throw a lasso.

He told me so much about this talking horse I almost started to believe him, till I asked him, which is all he was waiting for, what Mr Turner and the other hands thought about such an astonishing animal. He looked at me as if I was out of my mind and said,

'Come on, Sissy, I ain't told Mr Turner about that horse. If he knew that old Paint could holler and throw lasso, he wouldn't have much cause to pay me wages to set on his back now, would he?' And Nate looked at me, crossed his eyes, and laughed down to his belly.

Other times we would just sit quiet on the rock, watching the river go by or looking up at the blue sky or the stars. We could sit there for hours, not speaking or needing to speak, holding hands or with my arm linked in his, both enjoying the peace and restfulness that neither of us had known so much of in our lives.

I remember one night we were sitting that way, it was warm and darkness was gathering around us, and Nate suddenly broke the silence. Almost in a whisper he said,

'Whenever I find peace I can never make it last, if I get too much quiet or too much on my own, even at night in my bunk, I get to feel the rope around my neck as if they'd really hanged me, as if I'd survived the hanging like a feller I read about once that they tried to hang him three times and every time the gallows failed or the rope broke, and the law said they couldn't hang him if that happened, but he always had this red ring round his neck where the rope had dug into him.'

I had nothing to say, could think of no words which might comfort him, couldn't really imagine or feel with him the horrible thing he was describing. So I took his hand, squeezed it, held it in my lap. I could feel inside him a kind of madness, like his mind didn't really think he was still alive at all, as if he thought he had really been hanged that morning so long ago and had moved through the world of men and women ever since like a ghost, touching nothing, affecting nothing, feeling neither terror nor warmth. It was an awful, chilling hopelessness that seemed to squat inside him, a hopelessness for the world and his place in it, but most of all, beyond that, a hopelessness that made him ache for a soul he felt he'd lost or never had.

At the time I wanted only to share and soothe his sadness, as he had surely soothed mine, but now I know I should have learnt from what I felt in him, that if I'd paid it more mind, if only I'd been older and known more of the world, then maybe I would have understood, and in my understanding found it in myself to help Nate grow again, to help him be whole. But I couldn't be what I wasn't ready to be, and so Nate was lost.

I can see it now, looking back on the way Nate was, that the way he treated me, the way he ran from Swann and lied to Marianne, the way he left me and Ma to do the planting, all the things he'd done to let us down, all the disappointments I'd had in him, that all these things were caused by this feeling he had that he wasn't really there, that he had lost his life when he had killed his Pa. This feeling would sometimes make him hate others when they'd done him no harm, or fear them when he or those he loved needed his courage. It caused him to lie and maybe even cheat and steal, I didn't know, and to put away the guilt he'd feel at those things, stand back from it and pretend he didn't feel it. It made him ache for the pain in me, I know, and even for the pain of those he'd never known or even seen, like the anger and sorrow he felt for the coloured people in the South where he'd fought, or those he'd only read of, the men and women far over the sea who had to toil long hours in buildings full of

146

heat and noise and never saw bright sun nor breathed fresh air.

Nate could feel, he could love, he could hate, but he couldn't act. I never would stop loving him, but I knew that I had to make sure I never needed him again.

15

Nate's Gift

It was about three weeks after my visit to the Turner place that we heard again one Sabbath, early in the morning, the sound of a horse approaching over open country. I was in the yard hunting out eggs and looked up to see who it was. I knew before he was really close enough to see that it was Pete Anderson.

I watched him ride into the yard and climb carefully down from his horse, holding something inside his coat. James and Annabel appeared from inside the house and stared silently at him, as if they didn't remember who he was. I greeted him and he opened his coat to show a little golden-haired puppy that had all three of us crowded round him wanting to get a closer look.

'I couldn't leave you out here at the mercy of grizzly bears and Indians and outlaws, so's I got this here ferocious beast off his ma this morning and if you want him he's all yours.'

He passed the puppy to me and I held him close. At first he wriggled and looked mournfully up at me, but then he settled against my breast and was still. Annabel and James clamoured at me to be allowed to hold him, then Ma came out and she wanted to hold him too and to know all about him and where he had come from and if he was ours to keep. So we took him in the house and sat around the table, passing him from one to another.

Pete wouldn't take anything in exchange for the dog so Ma told him he had to stay to dinner. He didn't take much persuading. We left Annabel in charge of the puppy, told her to think of a name for him, and went back out into the yard. As the sun rose in the sky it started to grow hot. Everything seemed slow and easy, and I was glad it was Sabbath when we did only such chores as couldn't be put off. I was glad, too, that Pete Anderson had come by.

'I got another present for you, Mrs Swann,' he said, and I blushed, still unused to company I suppose.

'Oh, Mr Anderson,' I told him, 'the puppy is the best present we could have had, I'm sure there ain't no need—' but he interrupted me, shaking his head.

'It ain't from me,' he said, 'it's from Nate.' And he looked sort of sad when he said it, as if he were embarrassed to mention Nate's name.

'He told me to bring over some books he left behind, that he wanted you to have them.'

He pulled a bag, a heavy bag, down from his horse and laid it on the ground. We both hunkered down beside it like children and Pete opened it up. They were all there, maybe twenty books by Hawthorne and Scott and James Fenimore Cooper, others I didn't know. I knew I was ready to read them, too. I felt as if I'd looked into the bag and seen the golden light of paradise.

Pete carried them into the house for me and put them on top of a high cupboard that stood by the door of the room where I slept, out of reach of the children and the puppy. Ma looked, didn't ask what was in the bag, didn't say a word. She knew what they were, I suppose, and she didn't like it, but she could see how happy I was and didn't want to spoil it for me. So she held her tongue.

Pete and me went back into the yard and I asked him if he'd care to sit with me in the shade of the porch. I felt so strong and happy and kind of full sitting there, I knew it was because of the books and seeing the children's delight at the puppy, but all these things became mixed up in my mind with the presence of Pete Anderson hisself, the good news with the messenger, and I felt so warm and good toward him I had to stop myself from throwing my arms around him like I would've if he had been Nate.

'I wish there was some way we could pay back your kindness, Mr Anderson,' I told him.

'It's worth riding over here just to sample your Ma's cooking,' he said. Then we sat kind of awkwardly silent, not in the peaceful silence that grew up between Nate and me, but like you could hear or feel both of us thinking hard for something to say.

'He'll grow real big, I ought to warn you,' Pete Anderson said, and for a moment I hadn't a clue what he was talking about. I must have shown it in my face, because he laughed and said,

'The dog there. He'll grow real big,' and I laughed too.

'I guess so,' I said, then lapsed again into silence.

I wished Ma would come out, who was so good at getting him to talk. I thought how Ma had seen some of the world, just as he had, and how dull he must find me. It seemed mean of her to leave us on our own, knowing as she did how awkward I was sure to find it. I wondered why neither of the children came out, but guessed they were occupied with the dog. I could hear Ma talking to them, cooing to the puppy.

'You looked mighty happy when you saw those books,' he said. I nodded. 'I always wished I could read and write,' he went on, 'but I never got the chance to go to school.'

'You can't read?' I let it out, surprised sounding, then

150

realised it might seem impolite and hurtful, but Mr Anderson didn't seem to mind.

'No, ma'am,' he said, but then added, 'well, maybe just a little.'

'I'm surprised Nate didn't teach you.'

For some reason, maybe at the mention of Nate, he looked embarrassed again.

'Well, Nate did teach me some, but we didn't get so far with it, you know. And now I ain't got nobody to teach me, with him being gone up to Oregon.'

He still seemed embarrassed, and looked as if he would rather be someplace else. I wished I hadn't mentioned Nate, who'd let Pete Anderson down as well as me and Ma, and who he obviously felt badly toward. I cursed my lack of experience, my lack of knowledge of the simplest things. I had no friends and no way of making any. I supposed Pete Anderson must be wishing he had never agreed to stay to dinner, and that he would ride away now and I'd never see him again. Then he said,

'Maybe you could show me now, that is if you don't mind and if you've got something real easy to read.'

This was, I saw straight away, the perfect way out for me. I had nothing to say, felt dull and ashamed, but it was true I could read well, I had started to teach Annabel, and if Mr Anderson couldn't read so well then that evened things up between us, at least a little.

'Why, I'd be delighted to help you that way, Mr Anderson,' I told him, 'after all your kindness to us.' And I jumped up and went indoors to get the primers that I'd first learned from and that I was using now to teach Annabel.

Annabel called the puppy Wolf. She wanted a name would make him fierce and brave. He was the kind of dog that's thickset with a gentle face and long golden hair, so the name didn't really suit him, but we'd told Annabel she could choose so we left it at that.

I sat on the porch with Mr Anderson all morning, teaching him his letters. Once I went in to help Ma with the dinner but she shooed me out, saying Annabel was all the help she needed and I had to look after 'our guest'. The phrase sounded odd in her mouth, Pete Anderson being the first one we'd had for so long. I told her I'd take James out with me but she said he was needed to watch the puppy. So I went back out and continued the lesson.

At dinner Annabel said,

'Is Mamma teaching you to read, Mr Anderson?'

'She has been this morning, Annabel,' he told her.

'She's teaching me, too, aren't you, Mamma?'

I nodded, feeling a little embarrassed for Mr Anderson, though he showed no evidence of sharing this feeling.

'Are you going to come over for a lesson every day? I have to have a lesson every single day,' Annabel said, watching me and glancing at Ma to see if she was talking out of turn.

But Ma just smiled at her and said,

'Annabel can read real good, now, can't you Annabel?' which almost caused me to choke on my food, given Ma's previous pronouncements on the subject of book-learning.

'Well, I have to work on Mr Turner's farm just like your Uncle Nathan did before he moved up to Oregon, so I don't expect to make it every day, Annabel,' he said. 'But I sure would like to learn to read better. Maybe I can borrow some picture books off Mr Turner's children and teach myself.'

'Isn't there someone over there can teach you?' I asked him.

He shook his head. 'I know there's some can read and some can't, but there's no-one I would want to ask to teach me.'

Ma spoke up.

'Maybe Elizabeth here can teach you,' Ma said, using my given name to Mr Anderson for the first time as far as I could remember, and my full given name for the first time in years.

'But Ma,' I said, shaking my head and probably blushing too, 'you heard what Mr Anderson told Annabel.'

'Sure. But that don't mean he can't come over Sabbath sometimes. When Nathan was teaching you, you didn't get to see him every day, nor nothing like it.'

'Well, thank you, Mrs Holt,' he said, 'but I couldn't just come over here, take up Mrs Swann's time and eat your food without giving nothing back.'

Ma laughed.

'You already given us something, and he'll eat more than you would anyway. But don't worry, we'll find ways you can earn your dinner. There's always some durned thing needs moving or lifting around here, that a man's back would be welcome help for. That is if you don't mind taking a risk that the Lord ain't so fussy over Sabbath here as He was back East.'

He was quiet for a moment, seeming to consider.

'Well I guess if Mrs Swann don't mind . . . '

I shook my head.

'It'd be a pleasure,' I told him, though I felt sick with nervousness at the thought of having to see someone so often, someone who wasn't Ma or Nate or Annabel or James, someone from outside my life, from the world.

He opened his mouth to speak, but Ma got in first.

'Good,' she said, 'then that's settled. Annabel, help me with the dishes, then we'll show Wolf round the farm.'

16

Gold in the Water

Pete Anderson came by every week after that. He seemed
to learn fast, and I enjoyed his company, looked forward
to Sabbath and the sound of his horse approaching in the
morning. Summer moved on, and Pete told Ma he would
ask Mr Turner if he could take a few days out and help us
with the harvest.

Every time he came he would find ways of helping us. He
was full of ideas, too, for how we could make money from
things we grew or made. When he heard about the gloves he
took a pair and came back with orders from all the men he
worked with, so that Ma was kept busy getting them ready
for the fall. In some ways he was like Nate, always fooling
around, making things to amuse the children, teaching the
puppy tricks, telling tall stories. But though I never felt easy
with him, never felt calm like I did around Nate most times,
I began to look forward to his visits more even than I had
looked forward to seeing Nate, who was my own brother.
Nate had left us, deserted us if the truth of it was spoke, and
Pete Anderson seemed sent by Providence to keep me from
the despair of that.

I never thought of him as courting me, I suppose because
I had no way of knowing what courting was. Swann wooed
me the way a mountain lion courts a faun. Pete was kind

and gentle and I quickly came to think of him as my friend, the first one outside the family I'd ever had, though Mr and Mrs Packer from the trading boat had shown me kindness. I no more thought of wanting another man, in the way that a woman is in nature inclined, than I thought of wanting to lay down naked in a bed of ice. I had held my children close and hidden in my mother's arms and clung to Nate as you might cling to a log in a flood, and all of these things had made me warm, comforted me, sheltered me from pain. I loved them all and hadn't known love from no-one else. Nothing in my experience then could have allowed me to see any connection between the terror that Swann had made me suffer, in his hate and lust, and the idea of love.

So when Pete Anderson came calling every Sabbath in his best clothes, with his hair sleeked down with oil and his boots polished high, I did not know what Ma knew and what I think even Annabel knew, that Pete had more thoughts for the teacher than the lesson. And either because of his own shyness – which I never thought on, being as he seemed to me to have seen the world and dealt with it – or because he could feel in me or knew from what Nate had told him that I had reason to fear men, he gave me no cause to believe he wanted more than my friendship. Not once did he touch me, though perhaps sometimes when we were at our letters he might lean close to get a better look, his arm might brush mine, his face close enough for me to feel the heat of it. If I ever thought beyond, though, it was only to feel a pang of guilty regret that he wasn't Nate, that I couldn't stand inside his arms and feel my troubles melt away like demons from a dream.

I never felt this urge so strong as when we would sit together on the riverbank near Tennant's Rock, close to where I had been used to sit with Nate. Sometimes we would go down before we ate, take our books and have our lesson while the Sacramento flowed by us on its long journey down the valley. Or we would take a stroll down after dinner with Annabel, who seemed to take to Mr Anderson straight away. James, who was always jealous of anyone or anything took my attention away from him, would stay with Ma, though he'd always scream to come with us and I would feel guilty and tell her to let him come.

'It ain't the best thing him playing by the river,' Ma would always say, 'even with the three of you to watch him. He'll be fine with me.'

I felt shy of being alone or near alone with Mr Anderson like that, but I didn't have no-one except Ma to tell me what was or wasn't seemly, so didn't think nothing of it. He never tried to sweet-talk me, seeming to be as awkward when we were alone as ever I was. There were always long silences in our conversations, though as we got to know each other better the silences became less troublesome. It was then, often, that I would feel inclined to lean against him and have him put his arm around me, feel the strong need to be touched that I guess is in most every warm-blooded animal that hasn't had its nature torn from it by something evil. I never thought of this any different to how I thought of it with Nate, least if I did the thought was buried deep in my mind where I couldn't see it.

We would sit, quiet, maybe alone or with Annabel close by to us, picking flowers or playing some game she'd dreamed up. She was always happy to do that, only interrupting conversation or thoughts now and again, maybe to show you a flower she'd found or a little bug she would hold in her hand without the slightest fear or revulsion. Annabel was always that way with small creatures, she seemed to love and care for most anything that lived.

Pete liked to talk, though. The silences got easier and I came to feel easy with them, but Pete Anderson, easier or not, was always looking to fill them. He liked to talk about his work, the farm, to ask me about my life. There wasn't much I could tell him, and though he talked a lot he never told me much more about his past, at least nothing you could fit together into a story. We were content, anyway, as Nate and I had been before, in the knowledge that we had both suffered and could now enjoy at least a moment's peace.

He liked stories, too, not just funny stories like Nate used to tell, but things that sounded like they come out of Ma's fairy tales. Watching the sunlight catching the water, he laughed to hisself and said,

'Tim Sykes told me one time that all the water of the world had gold in it, and that you could see it when the sun shone that way. The only trick was knowing how to get it out. Trouble was, human fingers couldn't mesh a pan fine enough to strain that gold out. There was elves could do it, but they kept the secret to themselves.'

I looked at the sunlight.

'Did he tell you stories when you was a boy?' I asked.

'Sure,' he said, 'only I never really knew they was stories. It wasn't like I was a dumb kid didn't know they was only fairies in tall tales, but everything Tim told me seemed to have a point. Like the thing about the gold. I think Tim was trying to tell me to look for valuable things in ordinary places, something like that maybe.' And Pete went quiet, as if he had embarrassed hisself by talking of such things.

'When you can read real good,' I told him, 'you'll see things like that in books all the time.' I felt excited having someone to talk to that way again. 'Say if in a book, the story had a man looking through mud or dirt to find gold, the way I've heard they do, it's always meant to tell you something about how to live your life, like say how you had to turn over a lot of unpleasant or worthless things before you found anything was valuable, except the person that told the story wouldn't mean valuable like gold or silver, not just that anyway, but valuable like,' I tried hard to think of an example, 'like a good friend.'

I blushed after I said that, but Pete smiled at Annabel playing by him and said,

'Sure, that's it, or that the best of things can sometimes come from the worst of things. Tim was always telling me stories meant things like that, sometimes about animals that would tell you something like, if you is vain and too full of yourself you are going to get your comeuppance.' He searched his mind.

'There was one where a fox tells a crow she has the most beautiful singing voice he ever heard—'

'And the crow has some cheese, and she sings and out drops the cheese—' I cried out.

'And the fox grabs it for his dinner—'

'And the silly old crow goes hungry!'

We were both shouting by the end of this, excited to find we knew the same story, laughing with each other in the high happiness I'd hardly ever known before, of finding another creature who knew what you knew, who you didn't have to explain every little thing to, who just knew. And I thought this is what it must be like, almost as good as that sister I'd longed for, a friend of my own who cared about me and wanted to spend time with me when he could've been spending it with most anyone.

Annabel heard us laughing and crying out and wanted to know the story. So we told it to her, and tried to think of others we knew. There was one with the hare and the other creature, neither of us could remember what it was, something moved kind of slow. We racked our brains over it, but I couldn't recall and all Pete could come up with was 'a Sunday morning cowpoke'. So we decided on a snail, even though we knew it weren't exactly right.

We told the story to Annabel, told it together, each adding things to what the other remembered, of how the hare got to thinking it was going to be so easy to beat the snail, and he took too long a rest and the snail won the race and of course Annabel got all excited over it.

'The race goes to the worthy, it don't always go to the swift,' I told her, 'that's what your Grandma says it says in the Good Book, Annabel.'

'That's right,' Pete said, 'and the Bible, that has stories in it too that are meant to tell you how to live,' he laughed, 'but I don't guess Tim was too big on church-learning.'

I remember another day when the three of us took Wolf down to Tennant's Creek to teach him how to swim, but when we got there he didn't like the looks of the water at all, and he looked at us so mournful and scared we didn't have the heart to put him in.

'When I was a little girl,' I told Annabel, 'we used to bring our dog Pirate, who died before you were born, and he would swim right across the creek and back and up and down it, he was the best swimmer I ever saw. And when Wolf is growed, you watch him, he'll swim this creek like a fish.'

I had to admit, though, looking at Wolf pulling hisself away from the water, it was hard to believe.

'I always wanted to be near water,' Pete said, and Annabel asked him if he could swim.

'Sure I can,' he told her. 'Annabel, you get your Mamma or your Grandma to make you something light to wear, to cover you up without weighing you down, and I'll show you how it's done, if your Mamma don't mind.'

'Can't you teach Mamma too?' Annabel asked, looking at me to see how I would react.

Pete blushed and tried to think of some answer for her, so I said, quick,

'You won't get me in that cold creekwater. Me and Wolf's dry-landers, ain't we, Wolf?'

And then Wolf had run off toward the forest, chasing a butterfly or some fool thing, and we had to round him up and get on back to the house.

17

Feathers on the River

There was a book of English poems in the parcel Nate had
sent for me, but somehow I had never been able to get along
with poetry and so the summer went by without me looking
at them. I spent most of it reading *Uncle Tom's Cabin*, the
first time I had managed to get all the way through it on
my own, though Nate had read enough of it to me so that
I knew the story. Reading it yourself is different, but reading
a book like that is hard. I had only just gotten so good that
I could concentrate on the story instead of having to put
all my energy into making out the words. And then seeing
Mr Turner's maid had given me a face for Eliza, a beautiful,
haunting face that seemed to hold in it such truth.

I was proud I had a brother who'd fought to stop that
dreadful thing. I thought how strange it was that he'd took
on an army to free Eliza's sisters, when he only knew her
from a book, but he could not take on one man to free his
own. Then I remembered that Eliza had no help, unless it
was from the Lord, as Ma would be sure to say, when she
skipped across the ice of the Ohio River with her baby in
her arms.

Even now I don't get along too well with poetry, and
though I still have the book that Nate gave me I hardly
ever open it. It was just that one afternoon at the end of

that summer, Ma had taken the children down to the river to gather some wild berries and I'd stayed up at the house, too weary of limb to go with them. It was the first time since Pete had brought the books that I'd been truly on my own, and I decided that I'd get them all down from the top of the wardrobe and take a longer look at each one than I'd had the chance to before then.

I left the poetry book until I'd looked at all the books I hadn't read or had read to me. It was again one of the happiest hours I'd ever spent. I almost forgave Nate everything for having taught me to read, and my thoughts kept turning to Pete Anderson, I supposed because he'd brought the books.

When I started to look through the pages of the poetry book, I noticed a small, folded piece of paper stuck between two pages. I wondered whether Nate had marked the page because the poem on it meant something special to him. I was pleased to see it was a poem by a lady and although I couldn't make out all of its meaning I felt I knew what truths it spoke, and I could see the lady who wrote it and feel her yearning. I can still remember the first verse, Gone were but the Winter, Come were but the Spring, I would go to a covert, Where the birds sing. It made me think of sitting down by the Sacramento waiting for Nate, and the long spells in winter when I wouldn't see him at all, and how he had gone from me but led me to a good friend to make up the loss in some part.

I sat awhile, thinking about this poem and the way it made me want to dance with joy and cry with sorrow all at the same time, something like when I knew that Swann had finally gone, or when Nate told me he had found a sweetheart and was going to marry her. Then I wondered if Nate had written something about the poem on the folded piece of paper, and I opened it.

I saw straight away it was a letter, that it was addressed to Nate, and that I ought to fold it up and not read it. I don't know how to excuse myself for reading it, but Nate had deceived Ma and me so badly that I felt, maybe spitefully, I had a right to use whatever means I could to find out more about him, why he did that. Then again, I was just a girl, with a curious mind, and I thought I could probably deal with my conscience after I'd had the pleasure of reading the letter.

But the letter, though it was written to Nate, told me no more about him than I already knew. In fact, the contents of the letter were entirely unremarkable. When I look at it now I can feel everything I felt then, that I shouldn't be reading it, as if Ma might still come walking through the door and catch me, and that the handwriting has the beauty of something perfectly suited to its task, without frills or flourishes, a writing done lovingly and in no haste.

What it said isn't important now, if it ever was. It contained an account of a journey, impressions of Sacramento, some humorous anecdotes about a business transaction which the writer had been entrusted to perform on behalf of his employer, and a horrified account of some brutal sports which he had witnessed.

'Some fellows strung an old gander up by his legs, greased his neck and rode under him, trying to pull off his head. They thought this the best sport they ever saw, and laughed at the men whose hands slid off the greased neck, laughed at the terrified screechings of the poor bird, laughed loudest when they pulled off his head. I come away pretty quick, Nate, when I saw what they was about, cause this wasn't my idea of a good time and I guessed fellows who could treat a poor dumb bird so could find some sport with a boy like me who don't hardly have the brains of a goose, as I'm sure you'll agree.'

There was more about what passed for sport in Sacramento, some comments about how pretty the girls were, jokes, messages for some of the other hands, and so on. It was a letter from one young man to another, and although its contents were trivial it was almost brimming over with affection and something else, too, a kind of respect. It was dated November, 1867, almost a year previous, and it was signed, in that same finely crafted, precise hand,

'Yr.good friend Pete Anderson.'

I read the letter through several times. I was filled with confusion, even bewilderment, at the revelation that the person whom I had been teaching to read, or thought I had, these past few months, had been able, before our lessons even began, to write a letter which would have stretched my abilities to their limit. I felt I must have been born to be ill used and lied to, and like Ma when she called on God to tell her why her son was no good, as she thought of Nate, I wondered why.

I thought of the time I'd spent with Pete Anderson, how we'd sat together with the primer before us, him struggling to remember and form his letters, and how I had encouraged him, told him how well he was doing, how proud I'd been of my teaching of him. All the warm memories I had of the friendship which had grown up between us seemed to ebb away, leaving me thinking only how he must have laughed behind my back, told the other hands of the foolish girl he'd tricked into believing her childish skill at reading could be of interest to him, a man who had long since mastered the art.

I cried, holding the letter still on my lap, and while I cried I wondered why, just why, should Pete Anderson use me so. I had read in books of tricks played, lies told, disguises and falsehoods, but always there was some purpose to the deceit, some gain expected and prepared for by its perpetrator. But me, I had nothing, nothing at all, and yet the world seemed set against me. A man had come and torn me from my childhood, used me as a beast or devil might in the worst of nightmares; my own brother had betrayed and humiliated me; and now the first and only friend I'd ever known had played upon me what seemed nothing but a cruel and pointless jest.

I cried and cried, and when Ma came in, mercifully ahead of the children, I did nothing to conceal my tears. She moved to me quick across the room, saw the letter, pressed my head against her, held me so tight I thought my heart would burst for love of her, and said,

'What is it, Sissy, what does the letter say, is it that has made you cry?'

I couldn't answer, went right on crying, harder than ever, so Ma picked up the letter and stepped a little away from me, still with her hands upon my shoulders, to see if she could make anything of it. I suppose she recognised the name, Pete, which was written on the part of the letter folded toward her, and said,

'Oh, child, did somebody bring this while I was gone? Ain't he coming no more?'

But I just went on crying, trying to speak and shaking my head to tell Ma she had understood it wrong.

She sat down at the table beside me, reached over again and took my hand, and said,

'Sissy, maybe we ought to give this place up and go some place to find work. There seems to be some kind of curse on us here. I could've sworn that young fellow, now—'

I turned to her, interrupted her, still shaking my head and sobbing a little,

'It ain't that, Ma, it ain't that Mr Anderson wrote me he ain't coming here. Look here,' and I took the letter back from her, 'this letter's written to Nate,' I pointed to his name, which I knew she'd recognise, 'and it was written a year ago. He lied to me, Ma, just like Nate did, he told me a lie, he said he couldn't read none and here's a letter written as well as any letter could be, and it was written before he ever come out here.' And I started again to cry.

I wanted Ma to hold me tight to her again, and I couldn't stop my tears even though I was afraid for the children to see me that way. But Ma didn't move straight away. I heard her say,

'Sissy, let me get this right, you're saying Pete Anderson didn't need you to teach him to read?'

I looked up, the puzzlement of it all, renewed by Ma's question, helping me now to hold back the tears. I sobbed a little, nodded.

'He can read as well as . . . ' I remember searching my mind to think of somebody who could read real well, then borrowing a phrase from Nate, 'as well as Abe Lincoln could.'

And Ma burst out laughing. She laughed so hard I thought she'd gone crazy. She laughed so much I couldn't stop a smile forcing its way out to my face, even though a late tear still rolled down my cheek. She laughed and laughed, picked up the letter, peered at it, put it down again, looked at me with my sad face and my smile fighting for the upper hand, and her laughter changed to the kind of smile she gave me when I knew, and I could feel it so strong, that she was filled up with her love for me, and she said,

'Sissy, you don't need to cry.'

She put her hands on my shoulders, turned me to her and looked into my face.

'Pete wanted to get to know you, baby,' she said. 'You ain't never known how a man will be when he wants to court a girl, when he looks at her and knows he wants her for his sweetheart and maybe for his wife.'

I must have looked alarmed, and I know I shook my head

and looked down and away from her. It wasn't that I didn't believe her, only that I was ashamed again that such a thing had never occurred to me, that I might be like the ladies in Walter Scott's stories, the ones who young men on fine horses yearned for, or that any boy who I might know could ever have such feelings, least of all toward me.

I dried my tears.

'Then why did he lie to me, Ma?' I asked her.

'Sissy,' she said, 'you are nineteen years old and as pretty as a lamb. Pete is eighteen. You act to him as if you think he knows everything there is to know, but he don't know no more than you.'

I started to protest at that, but Ma kept right on.

'So he's been to Sacramento City and he's seen miners and saloon doors and fancy women, he's even seen the Pacific Ocean, so he says, and I guess if he lived at Eureka he must have seen it at that. But he ain't never felt a child grow in him, he ain't never known your pain, he don't know the terrible things we know of, Sissy. He's just a boy, almost a man it's true, and he hears about you from Nate and what a fine strong person you are, what you have suffered, and how pretty you are to look on. Pete's looking for a wife, like I said, he's young to be doing that but he ain't got nobody, he's tired of being alone in the world.

'Don't be hard on him, Sissy, for making up that story. He's too shy, too unsure of hisself, to ask you outright if he can come over here, or to ask me if I mind him courting you. You mustn't think that all men are like Swann, that if they see a woman they just want to hurt her and use her.' She laughed again.

'It's like they say about grizzlies, that they're more scared of you than you are of them, but I must admit I've never cared to test that one.'

I smiled up at her again, still wanting to cry but stopping myself, holding myself tight inside.

'Pete lied to you because he's lonely, baby, he wants to come out here and sit by you. When you lost a brother and I lost my son over again, Pete maybe lost the best friend he'd had. It wasn't only that Nate moved away, but that Pete knew how he'd treated us and he didn't like it, thought it cruel. Pete didn't know, when he come over here with that message, that it weren't true, so he was lied to just like we were. Nathan used him like he most likely uses everyone. So when he started to come over here he was helping us all, he wanted to stop us grieving and stop hisself, too. Then he took a long look at you and he saw a strong, fine woman who could be his companion in life, work hard with him to better hisself, which is what Pete Anderson wants more than anything, and he saw too a woman who could turn any man's head.'

'If you're right, Ma, don't you think his lying to me means we can't trust him? Maybe he really wants the farm, maybe he wants to make me his wife just so he can get the farm.'

Ma thought a minute. She stroked her chin, slowly, and looked off into space. Eventually she said,

'I'm sure Pete sees a pretty parcel of land here as well as a pretty woman. We don't need to fear that. We need him, Sissy, like we even needed Swann. He ain't no animal. I think he will treat us fair, he would be a good husband to you, Sissy, and that don't mean he is St Paul but it means something.'

'How do you know this, Ma?' I asked her.

She smiled.

'Well, I've talked to Pete and I can see good in him. I've seen him work. I've known some men, too, and I've loved one and bore his children.'

She was quiet again. I could hear the children playing in the yard, the yelp of the puppy.

'You deserve something, Sissy. I can't blame Nate for all of it. I let Swann be here, do his evil. You got a chance of something, you can start out on life now, you still ain't twenty years old. Don't blame Pete too hard. You have come a long way relying on yourself, and I'm sure you could get further yet. Don't take him if you don't want him. But forget Swann, forget the hurt he done you, it ain't all like that. You tell Pete if he ever lies to you again you'll run off with an Indian, then you watch him courting you. It is something to see.'

And she laughed and took me again in her strong, beautiful arms.

Pete was due to come over that Sabbath, bed down in the barn and help out with the harvest. I knew we needed him, too, and while I hadn't made my mind up if Ma was right, or if we could go on being friends, I'd decided that if he promised not to lie to me again, like she said, I wouldn't do nothing to stop him coming over. I couldn't sleep at night for thinking of it, wondering whether what Ma said was true, wondering if I wanted it to be true, and wondering still what other explanation there could be.

When Sabbath morning came I woke up late, having been awake most the night, and told Ma I was going out for some air, if she would take care of the children.

'Pete will want to see you when he gets here, Sissy,' she said, as if nothing had happened between me and him.

I thought about it. I was scared to see him, like I'd been scared to see Nate when I found out that he was lying to Marianne about his past, but I wanted to see him too, and I wanted it badly. I was hurting from what he did, but I wasn't sure if I could stand to go back to a life without a friend.

'I don't know, Ma,' I said.

'Well,' Ma said, 'Pete's gonna be here two or three days at least, you want me to have Annabel put food out for you down by the forest, or do you think you can shoot enough to live on?'

I laughed with her, though I didn't feel much like laughing. I shook my head.

'All right, Ma, I'm going to take the path down to Tennant's Rock, and then I'm going to take the same path back. So if Mr Anderson wants to see me, you send him on down there and he can walk me back up to the house.'

I picked up my shotgun from its stand on the wall, the same place it had hung when Pa was alive, Ma said. Ma looked at me and smiled.

'At least I can tell him he don't need to fear no bears,' she said.

When I got to the rock I climbed up on it, just as if it were a summer evening and I was going to wait for Nate. I felt nervous and hollow, and thought that if Pete appeared I would dive into the river and swim as far as I could, maybe to the land where the King of the Sea lived with all his stolen wives. But after all, I couldn't really swim, or at least I hadn't since I was a little girl, and Pete Anderson could. He could do most anything, it seemed, certainly anything a dumb farm girl could do.

I looked at the trees on the far bank, stared down into the water and thought about the times I'd had there with Nate, the happy times and the bad ones too, the time he'd told me how he'd felt when he thought they was going to hang him, of the awful things he'd suffered in prison, and the things he didn't tell me, that I could just feel, the things that had grown inside him from the horror of having killed his Pa.

There was some kind of waterfowl gathering on the river,

getting ready to fly away from the coming winter, small, tawny coloured birds that when Swann was here and it was this time of year he would bring home by the sackful. I thought how pleased Ma would be if I shot a couple to save a chicken, but I hadn't the heart for it. I could walk back now to the house, pick up a chicken I'd fed these months and wring her neck, though I never liked to do it. Something was going to die, it's true, so we could live, but whether she was in my belly or pecking around our yard that chicken would stay put. Soon the birds on the river would rise up in a flock, their wings would beat loud and they'd blacken the sky, and if you stood and watched them long enough the great flock would be nothing more than a dot, moving toward the sun. And if I let go with my shotgun something of that dot would be left behind on the water, when the flock rose to wheel away toward the sun something would be left behind, some spark and spirit of the life of the flock and of the world, feathered bodies in reddened water.

I sat on the rock watching the waterfowl until the sun had climbed much higher in the sky. I wondered if maybe Ma had told Pete about the letter and he had been shamed to meet me and had gone on home. I realised with a pang that I might not see him again, and I eased myself down from the rock and quickened my footsteps away from the river.

Then I heard him. He was calling my name, loud, I could tell that he was standing in the cleared field just beyond the forest, shouting to me, 'Sissy, Sissy!' which he hadn't once called me before, and stopping me dead, not knowing whether to run to him or away from him, my feet like the donkey in a story Nate told me, when you put him between two bundles of food, and the bundles were the same size and exactly the same distance from the donkey, poor dumb beast starved to death for want of having any way of knowing which way to turn.

Nate's stories.

I saw him, Pete Anderson in his Sabbath suit, come for his reading lesson and to laugh at a poor farm girl who had ideas above herself, poor girl thought she could read better than a man like Mr Anderson, who'd been to Sacramento no less. And it made me so mad thinking how he had fooled me and laughed behind my back I walked as fast as I could in his direction, and when he saw me and stumbled toward me, looking foolish in his church clothes in the damp green brown of the forest, I said to him, shouted at him,

'I don't know how you got the nerve coming back here, Pete Anderson, after you been laughing at me,' and then he was right up to me and he said, out of breath as I stood my ground,

'Sissy, I ain't laughed at you, I only wanted, I couldn't think of any—' and then he fell against me, into my arms, and I realised that he was crying, crying real tears, then I was too, and I didn't want for either of us ever to have to move from that place in the forest, or our tears ever to stop flowing together on our faces pressed close and warm, I didn't want ever to stop holding on to him there, in the forest, in the morning, in the time of year we call the fall.

I remember walking back up to the house. Pete held my hand and it was as if all the pain I'd got from Swann was turned up on its head, everything in me that had feared and hated, all of my flesh and spirit that had cringed from Swann's evil, now craved and longed for Pete's embrace.

We stopped by the barn, just in the place Nate and me had stopped the day he told me about Marianne, and Pete held me again in his arms. I thought of my dream, and how this was the first time I'd ever felt in life what I felt in my dream when the tall, strong young woman embraced me and held me close.

Pete had his mouth close to my ear, I heard him murmur, low and quiet, 'Oh, Sissy,' and it took all my strength, took all the will I'd needed when I had to do what was right when Nate could not, all that had sustained me, it took more courage to break from Pete's holding of me than it had to stand the pain of Swann's lust. I thought I would cry again, and when I saw the fear on Pete's face I hurt for him, too, and I lowered my eyes from his face, looked at the ground and his high polished boots, and I gathered myself up, like it was one last effort and after that I would have him to help me, his strength to add to mine. And Pete said,

'What is it, Sissy?'

I shook my head. I smiled a little but I could feel the tears hot inside my face.

'No, Pete, not Sissy, not now, Elizabeth, that's my given name, that's it, Elizabeth, you have to call me Elizabeth.'

And I took both his hands and leaned forward into him again, felt him around me and heard him say it, 'Elizabeth,' and knew I would never need to push myself away from him again.

18

Christmas, 1868

I was Elizabeth Anderson by Christmas, married quietly at the Turner place, much to Pete's disappointment. He wanted a barn dance and all of those things, but I was scared and told myself it would only serve to remind me of Nate. I didn't want, either, to think on my dream, so I didn't want the wedding to take place at the Turners' house at all, but Pete said this would happen whenever a hand or a serving girl married – they usually wed each other, anyway – and that Mr Turner had been good to him and expected it of him. Ma didn't come, she stayed home with the children, but I didn't mind that, either. I knew she wanted the wedding to go ahead, she was just scared of going back into the world after all that time. And someone had to see to Annabel and James.

We'd never had Christmas. Ma's folks never bothered with it, they'd moved to Ohio from Massachusetts, where such things weren't approved, and I hardly knew of it except for Mr Packer trying to sell me candy or fruit or pretty things, saying,

'Why, Christmas'll be on us soon.'

We had no need or inclination to keep such close track of the days as we knew just when it was the twenty-fifth of December. It was the same with birthdays. After Swann had gone we had some good times, Ma would show the children how to duck for apples, or she would make candy and we would have a game hunting it, but these things come when it seemed natural, when we'd finished the planting or reaping or when the winter dark kept the children indoors. We always measured out the days to Sabbath, but the rest of it belonged to a world we'd left, or been cast from.

Pete changed all that. He would ride to Chico every week on the day before Sabbath, not to drink and whore but to buy a newspaper, do business, get things you couldn't buy from the boat.

Pete had plans. He said the railroad would soon be in this part of the country and we would be able to get to Sacramento whenever we wanted. We could grow things to sell instead of to eat ourselves, not just selling what we had to spare but raising whole crops, maybe wheat and fruit trees, selling it for money to the folks in the growing towns further south and using the money to buy what we needed.

'I've seen Mr Turner and how he works,' Pete said. 'He raises cattle, but he don't live on steaks. Farmer has to be a businessman now, Lizabeth, these are times when a man with some brains who ain't afraid of work can get rich.'

And so Pete would go to town and come back with the newspaper and books and pamphlets about 'scientific farming' and he would pore over them at night by the light of the lamp, while I read one of my precious books or the *Godey's Lady's Book* that he'd always buy for me.

Pete had Annabel counting off the days to Christmas. He told her Santa Claus was going to sneak in in the night while she slept and leave everyone a gift. He said even Wolf would get one, or he might bite Santa Claus and that would never do. The day before Christmas he hardly did any regular chores. He took Annabel into the forest and cut down a young pine for our Christmas Tree. James wouldn't go with

175

them. He wanted to stay with his Mamma, and she was busy making pies and other food that Pete said folks always had at Christmas.

When they got back Pete brought out a bag he'd had hid somewhere. He gave me some corn to pop and then showed me how to put it on to long strings of cotton. Ma helped me, but Annabel helped Pete with the tree. James would not help anyone, and I wondered if he was ill. He would cry at nothing and give me and Ma no peace. Pete gave him a piece of candy, Ma gave him some corn, nothing would quiet him for longer than it took to eat.

Pete put a piece of cloth, green cloth in the corner of the room alongside the window. He put a big stone jar on it, then packed the tree into the jar with soil and moss we brought from just outside the yard. He put some more of the green cloth around the jar to pretty it up. When we'd set the tree up we strung the popcorn on it, then Pete reached in his bag and brought out shiny glass balls, tiny looking-glasses, and little coloured bags which hung from the tree on strings and which it turned out were filled with candy. Pete wanted to put candles on it like he'd seen at the Turner place, but Ma said they would catch fire and burn the place down.

After we'd finished on the tree Pete helped Annabel cut out some pictures of Christmas from *Godey's Lady's Book* and we stuck them around the walls. We each had to hang up a stocking, even Ma who had to pretend she was 'too old for such foolishness' but was really almost as excited by it all as Annabel. Then I tried to put the children to bed, but Annabel was too wound up by the idea of Santa Claus and James still had a sour mood on him, there was no pleasing him at all. In the end they slept, and so did I. Pete pretended to, but unless there really is a Santa Claus he must have climbed out of bed after I fell asleep.

When Annabel woke us, when the night was still as black

as can be and we had only Pete's pocket-watch to tell us it was almost morning, the stockings had been filled with fruit and candy and nuts and everyone had a gift. Annabel had a doll whose eyes moved, you could take off her clothes and dress her again, and James had a little wooden cart on wheels. Ma got a needle book made from soft leather and I got a box of paper with three pencils.

Only Pete got nothing. I guess I knew there would be gifts but, never having had Christmas, neither me nor Ma really knew how to prepare for it, beyond what Pete told us we should do. He told Annabel that he'd forgotten to write a letter to Santa Claus telling him that he'd come to live with her, so Santa Claus hadn't known to leave him a present.

It was a day I remember, a day I started to feel married, started to feel that Pete and me and the kids and Ma were a family like any other. It was a feeling I liked, though it scared me, too. I hadn't had much, but the good things I had I cherished, and I worried from the first with Pete that he would threaten them, or that my need for him would threaten them. Or that maybe, like Nate, he would let me down.

That Christmas made me feel better about it. I don't know if it was at Christmas when Annabel started to call Pete Pa, it might have been before but it wasn't any after. I know that night she used my pencils and paper to copy a design off one of the pictures from *Godey's*, and gave it to Pete for a present, before I finally got her off to bed. James never would call Pete Pa, but even James seemed happy enough that day, pushing his truck around the floor and calling us all to look when he filled it with twigs or made it roll away fast.

19

Independence Day, 1870

That was a healing time, that first year and a half of my marriage to Pete, a time when we grew together and found in each other something strong and reliable, something you could leave in the morning knowing it would still be there at night. Annabel found it, too, and Ma looked to Pete for everything she had lost when she lost her own son. Only James kept his distance, demanding more of me, wanting me always to be for him and not for Pete or even Annabel.

I knew, though, that Pete wasn't fully happy, that there was something he wanted that I couldn't give him, some part of him that felt confined. It took me a while to learn his ways, and longer to learn to be his wife.

Swann had taught me only fear, a need to turn away and look inside, where I could always, even at the darkest times, find solace. My body still feared and Pete had to help me learn again the way to calm and comfort it.

But that wasn't the worst, Pete was patient and knew the pain I'd suffered. The worst was not when I found it hard to give freely in love what had before been always forced from me in hate, the worst was when Pete wanted something of my spirit, wanted to come inside the secret place of my soul where no-one else had ever seen. I tried to let him in, but the frustration he felt when I could not open those rusted gates was greater, I knew, than any pain he might have felt when I could not give back his loving touch. He needed, as much as I did, to feel safe inside my heart.

Slowly, I opened myself to him. The pain and frustration lessened. As our spirits embraced I found that I could lie with him and that the fear of it was gone. And then a new fear grew in me, that I would bear him no children. All through the year and on through the winter into the next I waited for the signs, and none came. Swann's hate, I thought, was speaking to me still, planning to drag me back into his pain, to rob me of the love I felt sure I would lose if I did not give Pete a child. How glad I was that Annabel loved him so, and what pain James would give me with his indifference.

And all the time I lived inside these foolish fears, Pete was working our land, looking out over it, watching the river flowing on down toward Sacramento, and howling with frustration. He never spoke on it, never put me under any blame.

He would come to me at night when my soul had been invaded by the dread of past pain and my body would shrink from his touch as if he had been Swann hisself. And I would feel his need for me and fear it, while Pete moved delicately from me leaving one gentle hand to stroke my hair as you might stroke a child. Or I would sicken inside and speak not a word to him in a day, his eyes would be hurt but he would go to Annabel and read with her, or talk to Ma about her life or about the farm.

Pete knew we were living through a healing time. He was younger even than me, not twenty years old in 1869, and the waiting didn't come easy to him. He never showed it, though. He had his own needs, I know, and knew how to measure and weigh them each against the other.

The only time his frustration would show was when he

talked about the farm. When I knew him better and knew the world better, too, I came to realise that the frustrations he'd felt because of me had poured themselves into this, that by allowing his anger to show in this one area he was able to protect us all from the strength of his need to have all of me, all at once.

It was the only complaint, in truth, he ever made. It was crazy to waste such land on corn and beans when we could be raising fruit trees or wheat, or running prime beef cattle or a dairy herd. Pretty soon the railroad would come and there was no end to what we could do, no limit to the riches we could have if only we could start to grow things that other folks wanted to buy. Mr Turner had started off back east with a spread no bigger than ours and look at him now. Only one thing stood in the way of Pete and Elizabeth Anderson and a fortune, and that was capital. *Capital* was Pete's magic word, we were all scared of it before we knew what it meant. All we knew was that Pete didn't have any.

I tried to comfort him, pointed out how well we got by on what we did have, but that just made him more frustrated than ever.

'You know what Mr Turner told me?' Pete asked. 'Never be satisfied with enough, that's what he said, and he was right. I want us to have a future, I want us to leave more than we found, for Annabel and James to know they won't never want. Things are changing, Lizabeth. The railroad's coming. If I had any capital,' he spat the word out in the same tone Nate used to say *Democrat*, 'if we had any capital or credit I could study these here magazines without feeling like a pauper at the window of a fancy store, I could study what we should be growing to maximise our assets.' And the last three words came out like, Ma said, a Roman preacher's Latin, and they didn't mean no more to me than that neither.

The only cross words I ever heard Pete have with Ma was

when he used to forget hisself and let the word *credit* slip out of his mouth. Then Ma would rail against him, saying he wasn't raising no mortgage on her farm:

'It's still my farm, Nate tried to take it from me and Swann, too, and if neither of them could then I'm sure no fancy banker that makes his living from the misery of foolish folks, no banker is going to get the chance to take my farm off me, least of all on account of the notions of a boy ain't even old enough to vote.'

'Don't you understand, Ma,' Pete would say to her, 'you have to borrow money in these times so's you can invest it, build your place up—'

But Ma wouldn't let him go on, she had heard his arguments and it's true they never changed, and she'd always tell him he could borrow as much money as he wanted. 'Sail over the Ocean and borrow the crown off the Queen of England's head, but don't you think to secure your loan with my farm. I got a paper says it's mine and nobody can tell me it ain't.'

The arguments never went on too long, because Pete wouldn't keep his side going. He knew she wouldn't be persuaded, and he didn't intend to go against her will, even if that had been possible.

It was the Fourth of July, the second summer after we were married, that the railroad arrived in Chico and opened for passengers. Pete couldn't talk about nothing else for weeks before, ever since the weekly paper he bought first carried the news. He was all set for going to see it, but more than that, he wanted us to go too. I was scared, never having been to a town since I was a little girl, but I'd seen illustrations of railroad trains and I wanted to see the real thing. The children, too, were excited by it and even Ma agreed to come.

Chico wasn't nothing, looking back, but it seemed like something to me. There were maybe thirty buildings of different kinds, but all built of logs. What I remember of them there was a saw mill, a tavern and saloon, a few stores, some workshops, a cobbler's shop, a little chapel and next to it a school. I think too there was a doctor and a store that didn't sell nothing but hats. The only thing I really envied them was that school, though I was making out well enough teaching Annabel and James their letters and how to count and figure.

We got to town in time for the parade and horse races. Rougher sports were kept out of the way, there being so many ladies in the crowd. The children of course thought they had been transported away to a magic land. Annabel was almost eight years old now and wanting to feel herself part of all the exciting things going on around her. James watched the parade, the horses, the preparations for the railroad train, his eyes wide, but he wouldn't leave his Mamma and sat in my arms almost the whole day, clinging to me and demanding all the time that I spoke to him, listened to him, gave him all of myself. Pete and Annabel had learned to cope with all this by now. It was a good thing they had each other.

When the railroad train arrived everyone cheered, a great noise for one used to nothing louder than a boat's whistle a mile or more away, and James cried and hid his face in my bodice. He was five years old but showed no signs of growing into a boy, he was still the baby to everyone. Pete tried to get him to watch the railroad train as it got closer, but he wouldn't. When he thought no-one was watching him he'd try to catch a glance at it from the corner of his eye, but if Annabel or Ma or Pete spoke or smiled at him he'd hide hisself inside me again, clinging on tight.

The pictures hadn't given me a real idea how big the

railroad engine would be, the noise of it and the smoke. When it moved slowly past us I was aware more than anything of the way the turn of the wheels seemed to make the pistons move up and down, though I didn't know if it was the pistons making the wheels move, or that they were called pistons, or how any of it worked. Pete had told me how it worked and Annabel knew from listening to him, she would ask him questions about it, but I couldn't keep it in my head. I watched the pistons and the wheels but I couldn't see how the up and down movement of one connected to the round movement of the other. And I couldn't imagine, however hard I tried, those wheels I could see now turning slowly round, moving so fast that I wouldn't be able to see them at all.

I thought of the boatman's toy, and saw in my mind the wheels turning so fast that the strange shining browns and blues of them would change to white, disappearing in a confusion of light. It made my head ache to think of it, and I laughed at my own foolishness, laughed with the excitement of it all.

I saw the great train move past and as it got close to me felt all of the sound, the cheering of the crowd, shouts of the railroad workers, the hissing and puffing of the train itself, even the unending voice of James, all fall away into silence. I couldn't hear nothing at all, it was as if I were alone in a world of silent, motionless people watching a silent train glide by with a movement so slow it could hardly be seen.

And then the train was by us, the carriages were by us, and I heard again the sound of the crowd, rushing like a river in my head, past my ears, past my body as I stood clinging to my son, felt Pete's warm hand on my shoulder, and as the last carriage passed I looked across the empty track at the crowd on the other side and there, just for a second as a section of the front row of people parted, I saw, or thought

I saw in the sea of faces, the hard cold face of Swann, stare straight at me, turn from me quick, then disappear as the crowd flowed again into the space in front of him.

I let out a little cry beneath my breath but Pete, feeling me tense through the hand he still rested on my shoulder, pulled me gently backwards so that he could see my face turned to him, leaned over so that I could hear him in the crowd, and said,

'Are you all right?'

I shook my head and held tight to James, shielding my face from Pete until a moment had passed and I could look up at him and smile. Then the crowd moved on to the tracks behind the train, stood still now in the new station of Chico, and we had to move with it until, quite soon, it began to drift away and we could make our way back to the wagon.

And Swann was gone, more completely than if I had seen him and then could see him no more, gone as if he had never been, or as if the chain of days had broke and fallen to the floor and there he had been, a face from a link on the chain long since left behind. And now, with Pete's arm to guide me through the crowd, and my hand holding tight to James, with Ma and Annabel holding hands just in front of us, the chain was mended and Swann was gone, back into the past where he couldn't add no more to the hurt he had given me, the pain he'd left to haunt me the day he'd rode off for good.

20

Fall, 1870

I could keep it away during the day, though I was glad it was summer and the dark hours short, but I could not keep that awful face from my dreams.

There I would be, standing once more at the side of the railroad tracks in Chico, the crowd all around me, and I would look up to the train and the brakeman would turn to me with Swann's awful eyes burning into my flesh. Or all the people on the train would turn and every one would have that face. And I would feel his eyes, then his hands, I would feel the weight of his body pressing down on me, smell his stink like rotting meat, hear again the poisonous, damning growl of his lust.

And then there would be Pete, holding me to him, trying to push some comfort into a voice filled with fear, holding me hard as if he would protect me from whatever evil thing had caused me to cry out. When I come out of the nightmare, looking for Pete's strength to lean on and to warm me, I'd always find instead a frightened need, as if it were Pete's nightmare, not mine at all. But the strength was there, between us, not in Pete no more than in me, it was something we built together against the world, something I could build out of my love for him, and out of the confidence I gained from knowing just what it was that haunted him.

No terror from the past, or at least not one that walked and talked and inflicted misery and pain; what frightened Pete was simply that he would wake one day and I would not be there. So, because I knew that this would never be, his weakness made me strong, and because he could at other times be strong when I was weak, I loved him for it.

The bad dreams came night after night after we rode back from Chico that day. For long hours I'd lie awake, listening for the sound of hooves or of a devil moving in the night, listening for Wolf's warning bark, listening for any sound that did not seem to belong to the air of a California summer after sundown.

Then at last I would sleep, and there would be Swann, and I would wake again with a cry, a moan or scream of fear, and Pete would be holding me tight, clinging to me with his own fear written big on his soul and in his eyes, his heart beating hard and quick. We'd rebuild each other then, two children after all, and Pete would sleep. I'd lie awake again until first light let me rise and start the day.

Without sleep I could not keep Swann off even in the day, could not do my chores or enjoy the times between. I felt James stretch me tight like a frayed rope. Pete, Annabel, Ma, they all understood and gave me space or filled it for me, as my need changed with the changing fears that had crept back into my mind and spirit. But James, the more lost I became the more he wanted me, demanded me, and to hisself.

It seemed to me all I ever heard was Mamma, Mamma, Mamma, and always from James. If I was at the stove, there he would be, tugging at my skirts. When I went out to milk the cows he would follow me, sticking his hand into the pail of milk, hitting the cow or poking her with a stick, so she would be fearful and restive. At night he woke frequently, whenever I'd finished the last of my chores and sat with a book or to spend some time with Pete I would hear

James' insistent crying, Mamma, Mamma, Mamma, I'm cold Mamma, I'm thirsty, I'm hot. If Pete tried to see to him he would push him away and cry all the more. Even Ma couldn't settle him.

The worst times of all would be when I'd lain awake for hours, terrified that Swann would come to me in nightmares, then when I finally slept James would wake and drag me from it again. Whether I slept or lay awake, the nights were terrible, I was dragged apart by the spectre of Swann or by the fathomless needs of his son.

And yet I never really thought I had seen Swann at all. When I'd looked across the railroad, caught the barest glimpse of that face inside the crowd, only in that moment did I really believe, with all my heart, that it was him. At the moment I looked into the face, saw those black and soulless eyes, only then did I feel Swann to be near, only then did the reality of him touch me. As soon as the face turned from me, as soon as the crowd flowed and closed around it once more, the certainty and the chill it brought were gone, there I was again with Pete and all the people that I loved.

As the crowd moved in behind the train, or drifted back up toward town, it became no more than it had been before that last carriage had passed and let me see across the tracks, a gathering of friends without malice or threat, people just like me who hadn't seen a railroad train before, but who hadn't either been beaten and used and forced to live in servitude and constant pain, women who had husbands and mothers and children who lived and worked together and knew the devil only from a book. Women just like me, Elizabeth Anderson, and nothing like the nameless girl she once had been. And the further we moved from the tracks, from Chico, the more days passed between us and that Independence Day, the less I believed that I had seen Swann.

So I said nothing to Pete or to Ma, until the bad dreams came, night after night, until I was too wore out to do my chores, until I pushed James from me, shouted at him to leave me be, and saw him cry and felt no pity.

And I lay awake through the night, sometimes crying softly to myself, until I thought I saw a faint tinge of light at the window. I heard the hooves of a horse ride right up to the cabin door. I heard the door swing open and smelt that terrible breath of Hell, sat straight up and saw in front of me, at the foot of the bed, the grinning face of Swann, bright lit as if a candle burned behind his eyes.

I opened my mouth to scream but no sound would come, I felt his hands around my throat and fell back, heard a voice saying, fearful,

'Elizabeth, Elizabeth, wake up, it's all right, wake up Elizabeth,' and felt Pete's arms around me, turned to bury my face in his chest and cry, cry harder than I'd done since Nate stole away and left me all alone.

My fear melted away in that embrace, a closeness so warm and true it made even the dark seem friendly, but I could feel Pete scared and in need of me, needing comfort from me, needing to know it wasn't for any loss of love for him that I suffered. I sat up a little and wrapped the blanket tight around us, whispered to him in the blackness,

'I thought I saw Swann at the parade in Chico. When we were watching the railroad engine. It scared me so bad I can't sleep, and when I do sleep I get bad dreams.'

Pete was silent for a moment.

'Are you sure it was him?' he asked.

'No,' I told him, not hesitating at all, 'I don't really think no more it was him. There was no shortage of men like that in Chico, I guess. I don't think it was him, Pete. But it's put him right back in my mind. If he ever come back I don't know what I would do.'

Pete held me, tighter.

'We'd fix him, you and me, Elizabeth,' Pete said. He tried to sound like we could do it, too. But I just didn't know, I didn't know at all.

I tried to move even closer to Pete. My eyes had become more accustomed to the darkness and I could see the outlines of the old chair and tall cupboard we had in our little bedroom. I wondered if it was coming on to sunrise.

'I'm sure it wasn't Swann, Pete, it was only a bad dream I had, like the one I had tonight. It got in me, in my imagination, I was thinking on him for some reason that day, is all, and I made myself see him.'

'You think that's what it was?' Pete asked.

'Sure,' I said, and felt him relax in my arms.

We lay down again, still holding close, and Pete fell back to sleep. I waited until the first faint light broke outside, slipped gently out of his arms so as not to wake him, and started another day, lighting up a candle to help the sun along.

The nightmares went away after I told Pete about them. I started to be able to sleep and Swann hardly came into my mind at all. We had long days of work and, when there was time, would sit together in the evenings on the porch, or walk down to the river holding hands and fool around by the water or read until the light failed.

Pete had taken to smoking a pipe and he would spend half an hour packing tobacco into the bowl, 'you have to get it just right,' then another half hour trying to light it. Mostly I remember that summer that way, always chores to do but feeling well and up to them, never letting them wear me down, and peaceful, being with Pete by the river or on the porch or in our bed, and needing nothing more.

Annabel clung to Pete, too, building her happiness and

strength on him, seeming to grow and learn as much as she had done in all the years before he came, opening like a flower at morning. James still wanted his Mamma, but so long as I got my sleep I could handle him much better.

Pete tried to be like a Pa to him but James kept his distance, watching us closely when we were together. He never seemed to take to Wolf, neither.

As Wolf grew into a big dog with long, almost white hair, Annabel and him became inseparable. Pete would take them down to the creek, teaching Annabel to swim like he had promised her before we were wed. Course, Wolf had taken to the water now as well, it was all you could do to keep him out of it. Except at night, and only then because I wouldn't let Annabel sleep out by the barn nor Wolf in the house, the two of them were almost always together, though as Wolf grew he took to wandering from time to time, sometimes going missing for a whole day, leaving Annabel pining and afraid.

James wasn't ever mean to Wolf, least not that I ever saw, but he hardly seemed to notice he was there. It was like Wolf was part of Pete, had come along with him in James' baby mind, and James didn't want to love neither of them, or to be loved. It was always his Mamma. I was scared by it sometimes, seeing what had happened between Nate and Pa when they didn't get along, but James didn't seem to hate Pete at all, or even to resent him. It was only that he acted toward him as he might to someone he hardly knew, not quite a stranger but not family, neither, certainly not his Pa. And even though it worried me some, and I would tell myself how fine it would be if James would take more to Pete, call him Pa and act more warm toward him, I knew that some part of me liked things just the way they were.

Annabel had needed a Pa, you could always see it in her, the way she was with Nate. She had Pete, now, and Wolf, too. I had Pete, but I knew enough not to count on having him always, even though I wanted that with all my heart and could feel strong in Pete that he wanted it, too. I had Ma, but if nature took her course Ma would go before me, and anyway, part of her was always with someone else, somewhere far away with Pa. Only James was all mine, and I knew he always would be. That was why I allowed him his ways, why I didn't fear too much for him. I knew we could count on each other, and there it was.

21

Winter, 1870–1

Maybe it was because of James that I wanted so bad to give Pete a child of his own, or maybe it was just the feeling that, so long as the only children around the place were Swann's, something was needed to give us a strength together that would overcome or just outlive the pain he'd left behind him. Looking back, though, I think I was scared of bearing more children, feared the grief it might bring as much as the pain I knew it would, and all that made me ache so to be with child was the knowledge that, though Pete never said a word on it, he wanted more than anything to see my belly swell and to know that he had helped to make it happen.

Pete loved Annabel just as if she were his own, and he tried to love James, too. He didn't have notions about blood, knew that folks must find love where they can, having found none in his childhood until he was taken in by a miner, a man without wife or any family so far as Pete knew. So it wasn't no hunger to see his seed made flesh, just for the sake of that, that made Pete long to father a child.

I knew what he felt, because I felt it, too. It was something to do with Swann, that feeling that in some strange way he still held us in a power that only a new birth, our birth, could break.

Though Pete said nothing about any of this, he went on

pouring the frustration I knew he felt into other parts of his life. After the Fourth of July he began to speak more and more about his plans for the farm, how if only we had some capital we could join in the great boom that was coming to this country now the railroad had arrived.

'I'm going to get it, too, Lizabeth,' he told me. I looked alarmed, but he said, seeing what I was thinking,

'Don't worry, I won't do nothing Ma ain't approved. She told me I could borrow money if I didn't risk the farm. Well, it ain't mine to risk, so I don't see that there'll be any danger of that. I guess Mr Turner might loan me some money against the next year's sales, if we went into the cattle business. But I'll have to go and see him, find out for myself.'

I let Pete do what he wanted to do, not having had any experience of such matters I didn't see it as my place to interfere. It was true Ma had told him she didn't mind him borrowing money. It was true the railroad had come, and I'd seen it, which I never thought would happen. Once I'd seen the railroad train I felt like I was living in a world where impossible things might happen at any time, so I didn't doubt that Pete might make us rich.

Pete rode over to see Mr Turner a couple of weeks before Christmas. I had been bottling green tomatoes and was wore out from it. Ma had gone to bed by the time I heard Pete's horse and Wolf's bark, but Annabel had stayed awake to see her Pa and came to the door with me.

Pete fairly jumped off his horse and ran up to us, only breaking his stride to pat Wolf and let him know he knew he was there.

He was all excited. Mr Turner had told him he might borrow some money next spring.

'But he wants me to go back and work for him a while.

He says he's had some problems and needs an experienced man he can rely on.'

Pete's voice was filled with pride when he said that, but he must have seen my look of worry.

'I'll get back here most nights, Lizabeth, most every night, Mr Turner says. And if I need to take a day off to catch up round here, that'll be all right. And he's going to pay me a foreman's wage, imagine that, and whatever I can put by from it, which ought to be most everything, Mr Turner says he will loan me at least as much next spring, so we can get that herd.'

And he picked up Annabel and twirled her round and round, while she squealed with delight, feeling his excitement and happiness, even though she didn't understand what had brought it on.

It was late by the time we had Annabel in bed, but we sat up even longer, sitting by the stove in the light of the lamp, taking joy in each other's company. Pete was full of his plans for the future, wanted to talk. I didn't really take it all in when he told me of stock levels and grazing and where he would fence and what crops we would grow, but I got caught up in the excitement of his words and felt myself swinging wildly between that and a cold, fearful sort of feeling down in my gut.

I didn't want to spoil his mood, didn't want, not then, not that night at least, to bring him down from the clouds, but small fears gnawed at me and would not let me fly up there with him.

'Are you sure about all this, Pete?' I asked. The question seemed to stop him in midstream, pull him down a little toward me, to where I could see him again.

'Sure about what, Lizabeth?' he said, puzzled, making, as he always did, more of my fears than I had made myself.

'I don't know exactly, Pete,' I said, 'but I wonder, maybe,

whether we couldn't be as happy if we went on just as we are. We have plenty of land when you count it all, and by the time Ma is old Annabel and James will be growed up. Maybe we could just go on like that, we always have had enough here to live well, so long as there's been hands to do the work.'

'It ain't enough, though, for all that,' Pete said, and his voice took on again that tone I'd come to know so well, the tone he always used when he was talking about his plans, almost like a preacher warning you from sin and selling you salvation.

'You have to think about it, Lizabeth. We're out here, we can live, sure, probably eat as well as most folks, if we work real hard every day until they lay us in pine boxes side by side.'

'I guess I never thought to do nothing else,' I said.

Pete's eyes shone in the lamplight, and he almost shouted back at me in his excitement.

'Well we have to think past that!' he said, so loud I had to tell him to speak quietly so we wouldn't wake James.

'Listen, Elizabeth,' he went on, whispering now, 'this country, California, is going to be the richest country anyone ever knew. I want us to be part of that.'

'I got all the riches I ever thought to have, Pete,' I told him, stubborn I suppose.

'It ain't riches I want,' he told me, considering, 'not exactly. What I want is, I don't know, just to be a part of the world. Look at what happened here, Lizabeth, look at what Swann done to you. Do you think that could happen on the Turner place?' I shook my head, not really understanding what he meant.

'How's Annabel and James going to make out?'

'They'll make out fine, Pete,' I told him, still not knowing what he meant. 'We got all this land to leave them, just like my Pa wanted.'

'Your Pa come west, didn't he? He didn't set around Ohio waiting for the grass to grow up through his boots, he got your Ma and Nate and he took 'em west, to where he knew there was good land and ways of getting it. If we carry on farming corn and beans, farming just to feed ourselves and not seeing beyond the next harvest, we'll be just like those folks who stayed back east.

'Listen,' he said again, 'how's James going to find a wife or Annabel a husband unless we do something's going to put us in the world, something's going to bring the world here to us, right to our door?'

I smiled. 'I did, Pete Anderson,' I told him.

He laughed, quietly, and reached over to squeeze my hand. He carried on holding it, looking hard at me in the dim light.

'Maybe you did, Elizabeth,' he said, quiet and kind of gentle now, 'but how do you know it won't be another one like Swann that rides in here one day, when we're gone or too old to fight?' His words made me shiver. He must have felt it, but he didn't let up.

'We don't even need to be old,' he said. 'Bullet in the back kills young folks just as dead.'

'Why are you saying this?' I asked him, thinking on those terrible dreams I'd managed to shake off, worrying that talk such as this might bring them back.

'Because I want you to understand, Elizabeth, that it ain't because I plan to be as rich as the Queen of England that I want to do this, it's just because I want to make sure we're safe from Swann's kind. I want Annabel and James to go to school. I want to get more land, move closer to town, have this place alive with hands and people visiting to do business. Don't you see?'

I thought about it. 'Nate told me, you know,' I said carefully, 'that there are those who rob you with a shotgun and those who do it with fine words and fancy papers. I just worry that if we have to borrow money, and I ain't saying Mr Turner is that kind, but if we have to borrow money, and if we have to find people to buy what we grow or rear, maybe we will have to deal with folks who know the world better than us and ain't too fussy how they use what they know. This life we got here, it's something I understand, Pete. I've done everything there is to do on this farm, men's work too when there weren't no man, and I understand it all, don't you see that? What you're talking about now, this is your world, I know, women don't have no place in it. How can I know what's right for you to do? I like it that we work together, that's all, and here this new life you got planned is already taking you away from me.'

Pete was quiet awhile, then, thinking on my words,

'There's truth in what you say,' he said at last. 'When your Ma and Pa come west, they left things behind, good things. It wasn't that they had such a terrible life in Ohio. But your Pa weighed that up and decided it was worth the sacrifice, that there was more waiting here. And now we have to do that again. Otherwise we'll be left out here in the wilderness, and there will be other men like Swann to destroy everything we've worked for.' Pete seemed brought back down to the ground by the things I'd said, which I knew I had to do to him but felt mean to have done it all the same.

'Tell me again what we're going to do when you get the money from Mr Turner,' I told him, and I watched him open out, forgetting all the doubts I'd shown.

He talked about getting more land, building a new house near enough to some town, maybe Chico, for the children to go to school, hiring men to help with the work. All the time

197

he talked the excitement and happiness grew in his voice, till I felt it too. What he'd said about Swann had convinced me he was right, but I knew too that what had happened to Ma when my Pa had taken her from Ohio was happening to me, now. It wasn't that what our menfolk did was wrong, it was just that they did it, and we went along.

Still, when I thought about how Pete was going to raise the money it seemed a good arrangement, just like he said. Not that I knew anything of such matters, or ever hoped to understand them, and I waited until next day when he'd told Ma and I'd seen her approve it, before I locked those last doubts into the back of my mind and threw my heart and shoulders into Pete's plans.

Knowing if the plans weren't sound Ma would say no to them, and knowing if she said no then nothing would happen, meant that I could listen to them now without any real fear, and they sounded good. Pete seemed to put the love he'd brought to me and to my children into everything he did, and to listen now to him, his voice trying to stay low and quiet in the face of his excitement, was a joy indeed.

While I listened I tried to see in my mind what the future would bring for us if all Pete's plans came out. That way I got myself in tune with his happiness, and by the time I lay in our bed with him that night I had made myself forget the fear that his ambitions always seemed to make me feel, told myself how fine it was to have a man like him.

I've heard it said a woman will know when her womb begins to fill with new life, but I don't know now whether that is always so. It must have been six weeks after that, when we'd had Christmas and were into a brand new year, that I was absolutely sure, sure enough to think of telling Pete. But I can remember something of that night, I can remember that I'd never lain with Pete before and felt such a terrible joy that it was all I could do not to cry out loud for it, and that when he'd given me his seed I clung to him and wept, I could not stop the tears and did not stop them until sleep overtook me, holding me in a pool of such sweet warmth until the sun had risen over a bright winter morning and I woke to see Pete drinking coffee on the edge of our bed and holding out a cup for me to take.

Christmas came and went and the year of 1871 started. Even when I was certain in myself I decided to wait till I'd gone another month before telling Pete what I knew he wanted more than anything to hear. It was a good time, even though Pete was working away on the Turner place. He came home most every night, just like he'd promised, and he was so happy to be making the money we needed to buy a herd.

I'd decided before the end of January to tell Pete without waiting any longer, but he was, for once, away on a trip for Mr Turner and I had to wait three days and nights, burning with frustration, before he came home. I had thought it right and proper that my husband ought to be the first to know, and so said nothing to Ma.

It was long after dark, the children and Ma had all gone to their beds, and I sat reading a book by candlelight. I heard the hooves of Pete's horse, heard Wolf give his warning bark, and then one of recognition and pleasure, and then he was there, standing in the doorway, and I was standing there too, holding open the door and seeing him framed by night, weary from his work and from the long ride home.

I couldn't see his face under the brim of his hat, but I could feel something straight away wasn't right, and when he took me in his arms I could sense in him some sorrow. And I thought with pleasure how my news would almost certainly outweigh whatever it was on his mind and bring him back to the happiness we could always make together.

I poured him coffee and watched him as he warmed

hisself by the stove. I knew he wanted to tell me something, and thought I would let him before I told him what I had to say. When he spoke my first feeling was close to relief that it was so small a thing to trouble him, until I saw the tragedy of it and wished it could be something else.

I didn't ask him what was on his mind. He embraced and kissed me again before he spoke. I thought he would never open his mouth, but when he did at last he didn't waste no words.

'I have to go away for a while, Lizabeth,' he said.

'Again?' I asked him.

He looked uncomfortable.

'Longer than that this time. I'm sorry, Lizabeth. Maybe two months, till we're ready to plant.'

I guess I didn't need to speak. I tried to stop it but he must have seen the distress that came, not straight away but gradually to my face, felt the shock of a growing sadness running through me.

'I'm sorry, Lizabeth,' he said again, 'but it ain't so long and Mr Turner's going to pay me real well for it. When I get back we can start thinking about raising beef and maybe other things, too. It's just the chance I needed to get a stake to put into this place, and it's too good to pass over.'

'I know, Pete,' I said, as quickly as I could, 'of course you have to go.'

He looked relieved, maybe having expected to meet some resistance.

'What is it he wants you to do?'

Pete told me Mr Turner had acquired some land up in Modoc County and he wanted him to move some of his stock up there, being short of grazing.

While he told me about it, I made up my mind not to say a word to him about the child until he came back. If I let him know, I thought, it might decide him not to go, and then he'd harbour some resentment deep inside hisself, like a wound in your vitals you don't know of till its dull pain turns sharp one day and you remember the knife or the bullet that tore your flesh so long ago. Maybe, if Pete didn't go to Modoc County, he would look at our child in the years to come and, if we had hard times or if there were times when he felt hisself locked out of the great changes he saw coming all around him, he would remember the chance he passed over and blame the child for it. And so I kept quiet, even though it hurt to do it, and tried to keep my mind on how happy we would be when we had our baby and Pete had his capital.

After we went to bed and I lay close up to Pete for warmth, listening to his heartbeat and his slow breathing as he slept off his work-weariness, I felt the child growing inside me and thought on it and it led me to think on Swann and how the baby, when it was born, would finish him off, drive him from my mind. I wondered if it was really him I saw at the Fourth of July and decided that it must have been my fear that made me see his face in the crowd there. I couldn't see that he would still be around here without him making trouble for us. I'd always imagined he'd gone far away, maybe over to the coast and the mines, or down to Southern California. I could hear the wind blowing around the cabin and clung close to Pete. I felt myself drifting away into sleep but then woke with a start, it was all I could do to stop myself from crying out, with the fear of something beyond the edge of my mind, an open door or the face of a devil, forced back down into me as I felt Pete's hard, warm body close to mine.

22

Winter's End, 1871

In the mild winter weather I took to walking on down to Tennant's Rock, sometimes alone and sometimes with the children, any chance I got during the daylight hours. If I was alone I might take a book, but if Annabel and James were with me I would sit on the rock and look out over the water, not downriver toward the Turner place but up to the north where I knew Pete was. Once Mr Packer brought me a letter from him, but of course I couldn't write back. The letter wasn't very long, it spoke mostly of the trials and troubles Pete and his men had met taking those cattle up to Modoc, but I read it over and over, sitting on top of that rock on the river bank.

Apart from Mr Packer we had no visitors all that winter, until February was near out and the air was growing warmer, though the nights were still bitter cold. A fellow came by offering to mend shoes, and we were mighty glad to see him. Ma's shoes were about wore through and Annabel's were pinching. They cost a deal from the boat and I was for waiting till Pete came back and could bring some from town, but it would have meant Annabel having to stay indoors, being as she was used to shoes and had never gone barefoot outside of the summer. She wasn't the kind to want to set around the house, either. Ma and me had decided we might go into town ourselves but we didn't like it, neither having to go nor leaving the farm with nobody to take care of it. So the shoes and boots man seemed sent from Heaven.

He brought news, too. The boat had missed a visit, which it sometimes would in the winter, and we'd had no contact with the world for three weeks. He told us a gang of outlaws had been seen close by. They'd held up a rancher just south of the Turner place and a stage coach on its way to Chico with some payroll money.

'You don't want your menfolk straying too far,' he said. 'There's Indian trouble, too, Captain Jack and them Modocs north of here is cooking up a stew.' He must have seen me pale at the mention of a tribe with the same name as the county where Pete was headed, because he looked at me keenly and said,

'You got kin up there, lady?'

I shook my head, tried to think of what to say. I didn't think it was a good idea to tell him my husband was far from home.

'It's just talk of Indians and Indian wars,' I said. 'I got a brother up in Oregon.'

The man concentrated on the soles he was adding to Ma's shoes, then spoke without looking up.

'Oregon's peaceful these days, I hear.' He glanced up at me, quickly, and let his eyes rest on my face.

'You got everything you need now?'

I bought some strong boots for Annabel and brought him the money and a mug of soup. I offered him a shot of whisky and he asked if he could top up his flask with it, stead of drinking it there. I brought him the jar and he said,

'Your man don't need no boots mending?'

I shook my head.

The shoe man loaded up his things on to his mule and turned to go. He walked a few paces then turned around. He smiled, showing cracked and blackened teeth. He looked hard at me, that hungry look I knew from Swann. I wondered if he noticed the slight swelling of my belly, and felt somehow shamed and proud, all at once.

'Be seeing you again sometime, if I pass this way,' he said.

I smiled back at him and nodded, anxious now to see him leave.

'So long,' he said, and raised his hat. I watched him disappear across country, heading for the road.

The news about the Modoc Indians had disturbed and frightened me, though I didn't say a word to Ma. I tried to imagine what life would be without Pete, and shuddered at the thought of any return to those lonely, friendless days. I tried to close my mind to it, and sleep, but I could not. I was scared the nightmares would come back, and that Pete would not be there to chase them away.

As soon as it came light I rose, dressed and went out to clear my head in the fresh, cold morning air. When I reached Tennant's Rock I climbed up and sat, watching the water flowing by, the last of the night mist clearing from its surface. Over on the far bank, fog still hung, clustering around hollows where the trees thinned out and the land sloped off toward the river.

I was thinking on Pete, and what I would do if the Indians killed him, but other faces kept coming into my mind. I wondered if there really was a Heaven and if Pa was in it. I tried hard as I could to remember his face, but all that came to mind were the faces of the men I'd known best or seen most, Swann and Nate and Pete.

Swann's face stuck in my mind, not the evil, grinning face that had always wanted to humiliate and hurt me, but the last face of his I could be sure I'd seen, a face of confusion and maybe of defeat. And I wondered if Swann was dead, too, and thought how for a while after he had gone I'd been sure I'd never see him again, that he had had the look, as he strode toward the door without a glance at me or Ma or his children, of a man going to his grave. Then I wondered again if it had been him I saw in Chico on Independence Day.

I watched the river run past, weeds and debris floating and turning on its surface, and I prayed that Nate and Marianne were well and thriving, and wished with all my heart that I would see Nate again, felt the cold morning air and thought of forgiveness, how I longed to give my brother the real forgiveness of my heart.

And I thought of Pete, the strength of longing driving away fear and leading me into a dream that didn't leave me until the sun had climbed above the trees. I tried to tell myself, then, that I knew that Pete would come back. I looked inside, but all I saw was uncertainty, a fearful future where I might again be alone. And I realised that even when Pete came back, he was nothing but a man like Pa, who could die, or one like Nate who might take a notion to turn his back on those who loved him. But instead of pushing me back into despair the thought warmed me, gave me courage.

I leaped down from the rock and hurried away, back to the house where I knew the children would be awake and asking for their Mamma. I could still feel tears unshed behind my eyes, feel the horror at the thought of Pete's death, the keen pain of his absence. But I could look inside and feel something beyond that, something that made me stride through the sunny morning as if I'd just seen Nate and Pete strolling arm in arm along the path toward me. I didn't have a name for it, but I thought I knew its meaning and why it felt to my soul like the sunlight felt when it was shining on my face.

* * *

I hadn't heard the horses approach and I didn't see them until I rounded the barn. There were three of them, tied up by the porch, fine horses so far as I could tell but exhausted and somehow fearful, too. I thought straight away of the outlaws the shoe man had warned us of. I thought of Indians, too, but something about the horses, their saddles and gear, told me it wasn't none of them.

I stayed by the barn, watching and waiting, wondering what to do. If the men were outlaws, maybe I should ride over to the Turner place for help, but that meant leaving Ma and the children with them for hours. On the other hand, there wasn't nothing I could do alone, at least not without putting their lives at risk. I decided to wait, to see what happened. I clutched my shotgun, hunkered down behind the fence at the back of the barn, and watched the front of the house.

It seemed like an eternity, though it probably wasn't above a few minutes, before the door opened and a man came out. He was a small, wiry man with a moustache but no beard. His clothes looked worn and he had a nervous air. All the time he was looking around him, holding a pistol as if he feared attack. I guessed Ma had said our menfolk were around some place.

The man walked over to the pump and took a long drink of water. I was too far away to threaten him with the shotgun and, in any case, there being most certainly two more of them inside with Ma and the children, I couldn't think of firing on the house.

More minutes went by and the door opened again. This time a much bigger man stood on the porch, holding Annabel in front of him. He had a gun at her head, but was turned away from her, as if speaking to someone still inside the cabin. A third man, tall and lean with long blond hair, stood alongside him with a gun trained on Ma. As the big man turned back to face Annabel, I realised with a shock that I was looking at Swann.

Swann said something to Ma, took the gun away from his daughter's head for a moment and pointed it at her. Ma shouted,

'Sissy! Sissy! If you're still out there you had better come on in.'

I stayed, hunkered down behind the barn, trying to think fast what to do. Ma shouted again,

'Sissy! He says if you come on up here we won't get hurt.'

I waited another moment, wondering what else I could do. Then I pushed the shotgun hard against the wall of the barn and covered it in rocks and dirt.

Ma started to shout again, but I came out from behind the barn, on the far side from where I'd been hiding, my arms held high above my head. Inside the house, I heard James crying, but he stopped as suddenly as he'd started. I imagined him sobbing and snivelling, bullied into silence by the man with the moustache.

Swann left go of Annabel and walked toward me. His companion followed, pushing Ma along with the barrel of his gun. They both stood in front of me. The other man was much younger than Swann and so blond he looked as if all of the blood had been drained from his body. He grinned and ran his tongue over his top lip.

'Well, well,' he said, but Swann said nothing in reply. He stared at me.

'Get inside,' was all he said.

I walked quickly up to the house and went straight to Annabel. I tried to find some words of reassurance but could think of nothing, so squeezed her to me as hard as I could and then went into the house to find James. He was sitting on the floor in front of the man with the moustache, and when I grabbed him and held him to me he cried, hard and loud.

I turned round to Swann, standing in the doorway now, and said,

'What do you want here?'

He stared at me again, made no sign he would answer.

The blond man grinned and said, 'Just a little hospitality, lady,' but Swann growled at him to shut up.

I held James tight to me and stared back at Swann.

'We need a place to bed down a few nights.'

There was no threat in his words, no promise of rape or a beating or worse, but the madness was still there in his eyes, burning fiercer than ever, like it had already devoured his soul.

The blond man grinned but Swann did not. He felt to me like he had that last day when he'd rode back in here, tired and ready to rest.

'What kind of a man you got here,' Swann said at last, 'fills up your belly then takes hisself off?'

The blond man laughed, but neither Swann nor the other man joined in with him.

'He ain't took off,' I said, but Swann shook his head and the other two men grinned.

'You ain't never been much on lying,' Swann said.

I looked at him.

'You think you are a better man, that filled my belly then emptied it again? That holds a gun to your own daughter's head?'

He moved toward me, I held on tighter to James, who hid his face in me. I was expecting a blow, at least a slap across the face, but instead he nodded toward the door.

'You might've had a gun out there,' he said.

Coming from Swann, it almost counted as an apology. But I felt a hot anger rise in me. I was aware of a curious feeling, that I was scared of the situation I was in, scared for my babies and myself and Ma, but not scared of Swann – scared of his gun and his fists and the hurt he could do us, but not of him, not of his devil's grin or his black, fathomless eyes. I remembered how my fear of him had gone after he had made me lose his child, almost killed me.

Swann gave the others an order and they herded us into the room where Pete and me slept. Though they pushed the door closed behind us, I felt less his prisoner than when I had to share his bed, cowering in fear from him in that same room. I wondered about the window but decided that, for now at least, it would be watched.

Ma looked at me but she did not speak. I think for the first time in her life she felt absolutely helpless, that she did not have an idea what to do next. I could hear the murmur of voices outside, a loud laugh that sounded like it came from the blond-haired man, and then Swann's growl.

'Ma,' I whispered to her, 'where's Wolf?'

'I don't know,' she said. 'I thought he must've gone out with you this morning, but I guess he's gone wandering, the way he does.'

I prayed then that Wolf would stay away. If he came back they would shoot him, for sure.

We sat in the room all day, sometimes hearing Swann and the other two talking or moving in and out of the house. I tried to keep the children from the terror of it, told them stories, made them play games. Annabel was quiet, subdued by fear and by her understanding that James needed us all to be calm. Sometimes she would go over to the window and look out, and I knew that she was looking

209

for Wolf. I wondered if she understood that he could not rescue us.

James went between extremes, sometimes seeming to forget all about the bad men outside the door, playing just like he would on any other day, other times sobbing hard while the three of us tried to comfort him, or just to stem his noise by holding him tightly to us.

From time to time we would hear the blond man laugh, sometimes the other would join in, but never Swann. Once a furious argument broke out, but it ended in a sudden silence. Some time in the afternoon the blond man brought us corn bread and coffee. After that James slept, while Annabel lay quietly with him.

Late in the afternoon we heard Wolf's bark, out by the barn. Annabel sat up, her eyes wide. She stared toward the window, but did not move to go to it. I put my arm around her and I could feel her trembling, her heart racing. Wolf kept on barking, probably at the three horses tied up over there. I heard the outside door open and then a single shot, followed by another a few seconds later, then a third. I heard Wolf yelp, then bark, then yelp again, then Annabel started to cry and James joined her, and I heard another shot but couldn't hear over the crying whether it had hit the dog or not. Annabel, who'd been so calm all day, now began to scream. I held her to me, quietened her enough to shout out to Swann,

'Did you kill him?'

There was no reply, except a low laugh that seemed to come from the blond man. I passed Annabel to Ma, picked up James who was now crying louder than his sister, and flung open the door. All three men turned on me, the blond man and moustache drawing pistols and Swann leveling his rifle. I noted how slow the blond man drew, stored it in my brain.

'Did you kill him?' I said to Swann, ignoring the other two, who relaxed and put up their guns when they saw I wasn't holding nothing but a scared child.

'Get back in there, or I will sure as Hell kill you,' Swann said, and he said it mean and quiet, so I would know he meant it, and he looked at me, at the two of us I guess, with such crazy hatred that I didn't feel like arguing with him.

Annabel had calmed down now. Ma had told her Wolf was too smart to let anyone shoot him, and he'd probably hide out somewhere until help came. She stopped crying, but I couldn't get her to play a game or take a hand with James. She went somewhere inside herself, somewhere I knew where she could see Wolf's broken body, smell his shed blood and feel with him his pain.

I sat, holding James, watching Annabel and wondering what I could possibly do. Maybe we could sit it out and hope that Swann and his gang kept their word, holed up here awhile, then left us in peace. But I knew, thinking on the hatred in his look when I asked him if he'd killed Wolf, and the way his eyes had followed the curve of my swelling belly, that before they went the lust and madness of him would leave its mark. There was nothing to be gained by sitting waiting for the storm to break over our heads.

James had fallen asleep now in my arms and I laid him gently down on the bed, covering him with the quilt. I moved close to Ma, put my mouth next to her ear and said, low as I could,

'Listen.' She looked at me, scared, but said nothing.

'I'm going to find some way to make them let me get out by the barn.'

She looked then as if she wanted to speak, but I stopped her.

'I want you to wait until you hear me go out through the door on to the porch. One of them will be with me. Then

I want you to count up to a hundred, kind of slow. After that I want Annabel to start to cry, loud as she can, then James'll join in, you can holler at them, you know. Just make a noise, a natural sounding noise, and keep it up as long as you can.'

Ma didn't speak, but she looked at me scared, looked at me too as if she didn't know who I was any more.

'Ma?' I said, and her look softened.

Her face still showed fear, but something like a smile touched her lips. 'Careful, Sissy,' she whispered, and squeezed my hand.

I didn't have to wait too long. After it went dark the door opened again and the blond-haired man said,

'He says you're to come and cook us up something hot. We're staying here the night.'

He was looking at me, nervous, as if he was asking me a favour. Ma seemed to move to obey, I don't know what was in her mind, but he signalled her to stay with the children. When I left the room, James, woken by the man coming in, started to cry, but Annabel and Ma moved to soothe him.

I went out and started to cook. Nobody spoke to me or bothered me in any way, though sometimes I could feel Swann's eyes. Once I heard the blond man laugh and turned round to see why. He'd found Annabel's toy, the one she got from the boatman, and was twirling it round to make the colours disappear.

'Put that goddamn thing down and keep your eyes on her,' Swann said, but the blond man kept twirling the toy and laughing until Swann reached out his hand toward him and made a grab for it, crushing the soft frail wood of it in his clenched fist.

'You ain't here to play no children's games,' he said to the blond man, and looked at him with a mean stare I knew too well.

The blond-haired man said nothing, he looked once at Swann, but Swann fixed him with that awful gaze and stared him down. The blond-haired man looked at the pieces of wood littering the table and I turned back to the stove.

After a while I needed some water. Swann told the blond-haired man to fetch it for me.

'Wait,' I said. 'I need to milk the cows, too. They won't go the night.'

Swann told the blond-haired man to do that, as well, but the blond-haired man said he didn't know how.

'That ain't no job for a man, Baker,' the man with the moustache said, addressing Swann, and the blond-haired man grinned and blushed.

Swann looked at me, his mouth curled in a sneer. He seemed to weigh up. Without taking his eyes off me he said,

'All right, take her out there. Keep your gun on her. If she don't keep her mind on what she's doing, take your hand to her. She don't like that.'

The blond-haired man laughed nervously, his face settling into a stupid grin that looked left over from something. Swann carried on staring at me with his mad eyes, the sneer of hate still bending his mouth, twisting his face.

'I'll take the bucket, too,' I said, putting as much fear as I could into my voice, looking away from Swann.

I went back into the bedroom and took the bucket they'd give us to pee in. I smiled at Ma to encourage her and remind her what I wanted to do, and thought how it might be the last time I'd ever see any of them. I wanted so hard to embrace them all, but knew I couldn't without telling the blond-haired man, who was standing in the doorway watching me, that there was something funny going on.

I heard Swann tell the blond-haired man to keep a close eye on me, and him and the other man laugh. I came out, told the blond-haired man to fetch the lamp and a clean bucket for the milk and set out across the yard. Swann watched us from the door until we got about halfway to the barn, then went inside.

I walked slow, counting to a hundred like I'd told Ma. When I got to ninety we were already by the barn and I heard the commotion of Annabel's crying and Ma hollering at her, Swann yelling at them to be quiet. It didn't sound nothing out of the way, just the kind of noise you might expect from children cooped up all day. Then, Swann had always thought Ma was keen enough but he saw me as dumb. If he was looking for trouble he'd look in there where Ma was.

We stood at the barn door and I told the blond-haired man that I needed to empty the slops round the back of the barn. I waited until we were right around the back, put down the bucket, then said,

'Listen, I'm glad you come out here with me, I can see you ain't like the others, you know—'

I looked at him. He was watching me, a young man, boy almost, and none too bright. He licked his lips like he'd done when he first saw me.

'I can see you like me, too,' I said, and smiled at him. He smiled back, and licked his lips again, swallowing hard.

'You got to stop them hurting my babies, you understand, I don't care nothing for myself, it's just them.'

The blond-haired man laughed, stupidly.

'I don't know, ma'am,' he whispered, looking round him to make sure Swann hadn't appeared out of the darkness. 'Baker there is crazy, I don't know if—'

'Look,' I said to him, 'I don't expect you to promise nothing, but if you'll do what you can to spare my babies, there ain't nothing I won't do for you.'

I smiled again and watched him, his eyes drinking me in

in the lamplight. I took the clean bucket off him, put it on the floor, and lifted his hand to my breast. He stroked it with a kind of gentleness that I hadn't expected, a gentleness that made me wonder where he'd come from, how he'd fallen in with Swann. I let him go on touching me that way, then said,

'Wait, I want to empty the bucket first.' I stepped back from him and he let go.

I picked up the bucket, began tipping the slops into the pit we'd dug behind the barn for them. I could feel him looking at me, then his hand touching me, then I turned quickly, throwing the contents of the bucket in his face. The shock caused him to bend over, giving me chance to kick him, hard as I could, in the face, then jump on him and hit him with the bucket. I took the gun from his hand and hit him hard with that, too, on top of his head. He lay still.

I felt the weight of his gun in my hand but decided I was better off with the shotgun, never having used a pistol nor even seen a gun like this one. I put the gun in the bottom of the clean bucket and dug out the shotgun. Then I hurried back up to the house as quick as I could, fearing Swann would come out again when he thought it was time for us to come back.

My only real fear now was that either Ma or the children would be out in the parlour or that Swann or the other man would be in the bedroom. My plan was to burst through the door and let fly with the shotgun, hoping to wound both men bad enough to allow me to grab the pistol, have time to aim, and shoot them both dead. But I realised as I walked back up to the house that if the two men were not alone in the main room then it would not work, nor would it if they were sitting too far apart. I had to know who was where.

Instead of going straight in, then, I crept as quietly as I could round the side of the house and looked in through the bedroom window. Ma and the children were there, and neither man in the room with them. I couldn't risk giving them any kind of signal, so I moved back toward the front porch, planning to see if I could get a glimpse through the other window. Before I got there, though, the door opened and the man with the moustache came on to the porch.

I waited, frozen with fear lest he turned his head and saw me. I wanted only for him to step away from the door, widening my angle and coming just a little nearer to me. He leaned back slightly, said something to Swann, and stepped down from the porch. My shotgun was already raised, and I fired. As I fired I dropped the shotgun and pulled the pistol from the bucket, but before I could level it Swann appeared, his gun pointing between my eyes. I was beaten.

I could just see Swann's face in the light from the house. I couldn't see well enough to know whether his grin had returned in triumph, whether his black eyes had opened again to swallow my soul. I wished only that he was not the last left alive or unwounded, that I had sent him down to Hell before my own end came.

He took a step toward me. He said,

'You would've been all right if you'd just let things be and done like I said.'

He still didn't have that evil in his voice like I remembered, only a kind of weariness. I had nothing to say to him. I tried to think of Pete, but somehow his face wouldn't come sharp into my mind. I prayed that Swann wouldn't harm Annabel or James or Ma, though I didn't have much hope of that. I prayed, when I knew he'd have to kill them all, he'd do it quick. I wondered if I could shoot him as he shot me, but I was looking straight down the barrel of his gun and couldn't even find the strength to begin to lift the one I held.

I stared straight into his terrible eyes and heard a shot,

and then, unwounded, saw Swann fall like a pine at my feet and Ma standing behind him, a rifle levelled at where he'd been stood, pointing now straight at my head. Ma put the rifle up, walked down the porch and past me. She took the gun from the wounded man on the ground and then put her arm around me, guiding me past Swann into the house where the children were waiting, James crying loud and Annabel trying her best to comfort him through her own violent sobs.

23

Spring, 1871

All four of us were out to the field, cutting clover for the cows. It was a warm spring day, just right for a homecoming.

Annabel spotted him first, riding across open country from the road. Well before he got near enough to make out, Annabel shouted, 'Pappa, it's Pappa,' and began to run toward him, dropping the bundle of clover she'd gathered in her hand. We knew she was right, too, though I tried to stop myself from feeling anything until he was near enough to be sure.

I saw him stop, lean down and lift Annabel on to his horse and then I knew it was him, knew I could allow myself the happiness of it. I looked at Ma, and she was smiling. James went right on picking, as if nothing was happening at all.

Pete rode up, and I stood up straight, my hands holding my back, so that he could see. He stared. Ma lifted Annabel down from the horse and whispered something in her ear. They walked over to James, took his hands, and started to pull him away, back toward the house. He pulled back, tried to twist out of their grip, and began to cry that he wanted to go to his Mamma.

I turned and shouted, 'I'm coming right on up, James,' but he went on crying.

Ma dragged him away in the iron grip I could remember well enough myself.

Pete dismounted.

'Didn't you know before I left?' he asked.

But I only smiled and shook my head, felt a tear escape my eye.

He looked at me for a moment. I couldn't read what was in his face. Then he let out a whoop and threw his hat in the air, took me in his arms.

We went on back to the house. Annabel had told him a garbled tale of bad men and robbers, so I had to tell him the rest.

The blond-haired man had survived, he'd run off two days after we'd carried him back to the house from behind the barn. Swann and the other man were dead. Soldiers had come looking for them a few days later. We showed them what was left. We'd dragged the bodies out behind the barn that night, and before dawn some wild creature had found them and messed them up. We covered them with soil and rocks, intending to ride into Chico and tell the sheriff. But Ma fell ill, so ill that for a while I thought she would die, and before she was well the soldiers came.

Wolf come back the day after the killings. A bullet had grazed his fur, right on top of his back, but it had scared him more than it hurt him. Annabel wouldn't let him out of her sight for maybe a week after, but then he took to wandering again as if nothing had ever happened.

Pete had his capital, and when he heard what had happened he said he'd never go away again. But the next winter there was a drought, and he had to admit he'd overstocked our grazing. So he rode again up to Modoc County, this time with hired men of his own, and cattle of our own, too.

Ma and me were left behind again, to see the winter through. Annabel could work almost like a grown woman by then, which made it easier, though of course we had another mouth to feed. We called him Tim, after the miner was the nearest thing to a real pa Pete ever had. Sometimes it was hard, but just like Ma had told Pete, we got along.

24

Fall, 1901

Times back then seem far away.

Ma dead, though she lived to a good age, and Nate like a character from an old story people have forgotten if it's truth or legend.

Swann, stood above me then like the devil feeding on a lamb.

Pete was right, and this is why I know: if Swann turned up here now the hands would run him off and welcome the sport as a holiday, a break from their chores. More likely, man like Swann would come to my back door and beg a bowl of soup from Ho.

Ho would tell me about him, laughing, 'he look mean one missee,' he'd say.

James don't never write. If there's parts of the west still wild enough he'll find them. I was wrong, see. Lost him. Wrong too about Pete. Didn't lose him at all, though I might go a month or more without seeing him. Politics and business, but he does find time for me, I will say that, between the two. Maybe not enough.

Annabel, now, she writes. She's in Sacramento. Taught school until a lawyer caught her eye. Two grandchildren, and I see them every summer. They went home two or three weeks back. Both boys, Richard and Paul. City names.

Only Tim stays close by, with his wife Sarah. No fledglings yet. Tim works with his Pa, and when Pete's ready to take things easy he'll be the boss. I told Tim not to hold his breath, though he's ready for it now.

We had another, Katherine, but Ma said it was an unlucky name and she was right. Not a woman rich nor poor can have four and see them all growed.

I like to walk to Tennant's Rock still. It's the nearest spot to the new house where you can get any quiet.

The tawny birds come each spring as ever they did, though the riverboat's long gone. I never go into the forest without dog and shotgun, even now. We live in peace but, like Ma would've said, pride comes before a fall.

I keep Nate's books in a special place, a corner of the library which is known as mine. 'Better not sit in Ma's chair,' they'll say, or 'Grandma's'.

I never thought to be anyone's grandma and not feel old.

It ain't that I think he'll ever come for them, Nate I mean. I guess if we were going to, we'd have heard from him by now. It's only that they were the first, the first real books I ever had.

I have Pete's letter there too, the one he wrote to Nate that time. I keep it in that same place in the book of English poems, though I never take it out. Last time I saw it was when Tim was come of age, and I showed it him and told him the story as I'd done for Annabel and as I would've done for James if only he'd been around.

Suffering is not something to look back on, some folly of youth you know will never return. Swann is gone, but so are James and little Katie. Still we've built something, Pete and me, and if the things I feared for have been lost along the way, then so must it be.

The old house ain't there no more. We took the best of it and burned the rest, though the barn where I tricked the blond-haired man is still in use. I can look all over the farm and find old things alongside the new.

Fall's on us, but winter holds no fears.